The *Maggie*

The Imago

The *Maggie*

JAMES DILLON WHITE

*Based on the Ealing Studios Michael Balcon film production,
The* Maggie. *From the screenplay by William Rose.*

BIRLINN

This edition published in 2014 by
Birlinn Limited
West Newington House
10 Newington Road
Edinburgh
EH9 1QS

www.birlinn.co.uk

ISBN: 978 1 78027 249 8

First published in 1954 by William Heinemann Ltd

British Library Cataloguing-in-Publication Data
A catalogue record for this book is available from the British Library

Typeset by Hewer Text (UK) Ltd
Printed and bound by Grafica Veneta

www.graficaveneta.com

Chapter One

The pub known as Dirty Dan's is not in a fashionable part of Glasgow, nor is it particularly well known except to the dock workers and seamen who like to be near ships and water even in their leisure hours. From the low mullioned windows the hill drops steeply to the waterfront so that a man drinking at the bar can look down over the roof of the customs house to the wharf, and by moving only a few paces towards the window can see ships of every description on the cold grey waters of the Clyde. To a seafaring man such a scene is full of enchantment – the cargo vessels being plucked clean by swinging cranes; tankers, ferry boats, liners coming in from the Atlantic to anchor in calm water. Sometimes, by contrast, one of the tiny Puffers, the ancient boats which still manage to ply their trade, comes nosing fussily between the bigger ships to find a berth and, if possible, a cargo, and along the waterfront men who have lived and loved and talked boats all their lives nudge their companions and smile with affection and pride.

The landlord was an old sailor, but his first expression on seeing the *Maggie* was of incredulity. He had been swabbing the counter as he watched the Puffer coming in at a steady four knots, but it wasn't until he saw the wee boy on deck and the mate leaning against the stern rail with a coiled rope that he really took notice.

'Well, I'll be . . .!'

The drinkers looked up with mild interest. Two skippers with the initials CSS on their caps half rose from their chairs. 'What is it?'

The landlord pointed with his swabbing cloth. 'Isn't that the *Maggie*?'

There was a scraping of chairs and a scramble of boots on the floor as men crowded to the windows.

'It's the *Maggie* all right. Coming in bold as brass.'

'Never thought we'd see her back in Glasgow.'

'And isn't that the skipper himself, old MacTaggart, in the wheelhouse?'

'It's him all right.'

A foreigner, an Englishman from Liverpool, asked, 'Who's MacTaggart, and what's that coal bucket he's sailing?'

'Coal bucket!' The landlord planted two hands firmly on the counter. 'If ye knew the first thing about boats, laddie, I wouldna' have to tell ye that those old Puffers could be used for any job in the trade – anything. If it's coal ye're wanting or a few head of cattle or a wee bit of machinery maybe, and just supposing ye want it delivered to one of the islands where there's no port, maybe not even a jetty: ye don't charter a CSS boat – Captain Jamieson's here, or Captain Anderson's. And why not? Because they're deep-water boats. Ye'd go to a skipper like . . .' He looked down at the wharf where MacTaggart was climbing slowly, and apprehensively it seemed, from the wheelhouse; then he added defensively, 'Ye'd charter a Puffer.'

'If that's a Puffer,' the Englishman said, 'I'd think twice before filling her with cargo. Look at her now – half under the wharf. She'll be gone completely when the tide runs out.' It was true. The *Maggie* had tied up beside – almost underneath – a big cargo vessel. With her funnel below the level of the wharf it looked almost as though she were hiding under the stern of the bigger boat.

'She's no' so big,' the landlord agreed, 'for the reasons I'm telling ye, but she's a bonny boat just the same – or was.'

'She could do with a lick of paint.'

'Aye, and her boiler's half eaten with rust.'

'It's a wonder MacTaggart hasn't had the bottom out of her before this.'

The landlord nodded sadly at their criticisms. He knew that they had as much sentiment for the old *Maggie* as he had, but they had too much pride in their calling to pronounce her a good boat.

'She'd be good for another ten years with a coat of paint and a new skipper,' Captain Jamieson said loyally.

The Englishman pushed his empty glass and a florin towards the landlord. 'The same again.' He looked down over their shoulders and saw MacTaggart with the mate and the engineman coming ashore. They looked quickly to right and left before hurrying from the wharf. Only the boy was left aboard.

'What's wrong with MacTaggart?' the Englishman asked. He realised at once that he had spoken out of turn.

'Wrong with him?' They looked at each other awkwardly, as the question was tossed from glance to glance. At last it was Captain Jamieson who said, 'I suppose he drinks.'

'Who doesn't?' the Englishman said, laughing.

'I've seen him drunk three times in the one day.'

They drifted away from the windows, back to their half-empty glasses. It wasn't until the Englishman had finished his beer and gone outside to the 'Gents' that their embarrassment began to thaw. Then they drew on their cherished store of anecdotes and tossed them one by one into the kitty of laughter. The atmosphere warmed and was friendly once more. Coins rattled on the counter, glasses were filled and emptied, the sun played on the sanded floor.

'Wasn't he the one that caused all that trouble in the Kyles?'

The story was confirmed and embellished as the deep laughter bellied through the room.

'Well, I never thought we'd see him back.'

'He's asking for it this time.'

From his vantage point at the bar the landlord could watch the boat below, and as they talked he saw the boy, who had been left in charge, climb with difficulty on to the wharf, where he stood with hands in pockets, looking disrespectfully at the big cargo vessel alongside and occasionally spitting towards its painted stern. Two men wearing blue serge suits and bowler hats came purposefully along the concrete and stopped beside the *Maggie*. The boy didn't see them until they tapped him on the shoulder. Then he turned and ducked quickly, ready to run, only to find himself firmly held by the collar.

'There's trouble already,' the landlord said, polishing a glass.

'Police?'

'No. Two bodies in bowler hats – inspectors maybe.'

Captain Jamieson stood up so that he could see. 'Aye, they're inspectors all right.' He watched as the wee boy stood up manfully to officialdom. The hands gestured and pointed. 'Wonder what story he's telling them?' Whatever it was, the inspectors were not impressed, for they pushed past him to the wooden ladder and began climbing down to the boat. Speechless with this violation of rights the boy watched until only the head and shoulders of the second inspector showed above the wharf. Then with one deft kick he sent the bowler hat sailing down to the deck.

'The wee devil! Three months out of school and he's as big a rogue as the ither three!' The landlord chuckled as he moved along the bar. 'Wonder how old MacTaggart'll get shift of those bodies.'

He looked up with his business smile as the street door-bell rang, but it was only his barmaid, Molly. She was flushed as though she had been running, and there was a sparkle of excitement in her eyes. She walked quickly over to the bar. 'Ye know who's just docked?'

'Aye.'

She was disappointed that he knew. 'Ye've seen her – the *Maggie*?'

'Aye.'

She said, 'I was in Bateson's as they left the dock. They're coming up the hill. Maybe they'll come in here.'

Chapter Two

The men in the bar listened gleefully to the hum of argument outside. The crew of the *Maggie* were coming in all right. The swing door was pushed half open and then closed again with a slam, but the husky sea voices could be heard plainly enough through the open window.

'I'm still the Master of yon vessel, and I know what I'm about.'

Then a second voice, complaining. 'Then tell me this: if we *had* to put into Gleska, could we no' at least have waited till after it was dark?'

'We've nothing to fear from *any* man,' came from the Skipper, 'or woman either. We'll only be here long enough to find ourselves a cargo. Then we'll be off again. And if Sarah or anybody's watching for us they'd be watching by night. They'd never expect us to have the effrontery to put in by day!'

The swing door opened fully this time, and, like actors coming on to a stage, the three men entered. They came in with a grin, for they were all playing the same part, officers of a busy merchantman snatching an hour's leisure between trips. To complete the illusion they needed something more than confidence and a jaunty step – a call for drinks all round perhaps, but it was noticed that none of them seemed anxious to be first at the bar and that when the Skipper did come reluctantly forward he asked in a low voice for one half-pint and made no attempt to pay for that. McGregor, the engineman, apparently encouraged, also took a half-pint, which, on being reminded by the landlord, he paid for.

Hamish, the mate, was too busy to drink. Molly's bright eyes had drawn him irresistibly across the room to one of the cubicles, where she was making a half-hearted attempt to swab the table, while resisting his embraces.

'Och, will you stop it! This is no' the place for . . .'

'We're no' putting out till tomorrow,' the mate suggested.

There was a flurry of arms and apron. '*Stop* it! Ye canna come to Glasgow once in two years and expect me to believe you've any honest feeling for me!'

The Skipper turned with one foot on the bar-rail. He raised his glass to Captain Jamieson.

'Jamieson, me boy. And how's the world treating ye?'

'No' so bad. And how's yeself?'

The Skipper made a dramatic gesture of fatigue. 'Busy – busy. One trip after anither. Never a day to rest.'

'What are ye doing now?'

The Skipper and McGregor exchanged glances. 'It just so happens that through force of circumstances we're – just for the moment – without a cargo.'

'Would ye be looking for one, then?' Captain Jamieson was something of an actor himself. He asked the question without a smile, aware that everyone in the room was with him.

'Well . . .' The Skipper's hand muted McGregor's eagerness. 'I'm no' so keen. It'd need careful consideration, of course.' He nodded solemnly. 'Careful consideration.'

'What sort of a cargo had ye in mind?' McGregor asked.

'Nothing in particular,' Captain Jamieson said. 'But there must be plenty who'd be glad to use your services.' He looked round at his audience for encouragement. 'A fine craft like yours.'

The ferry pilot drank deeply and pushed his empty glass across the table. 'If ye weren't fussy,' he began, 'there's maybe some coal . . .'

'Fussy!' the Skipper said. 'No one can say that of Peter MacTaggart. Coal, d'ye say? Well, maybe as a favour . . .'

'Heard there was a cargo of machinery in 'B' sheds,' Captain Anderson cut in.

'Machinery? Now I must say, that's just a wee bit more dignified. D'ye know it's destination?'

'New York.'

'New York!' The Skipper gripped the bar with one hand. He drank the rest of his beer, and then, gaining courage, said firmly, 'Where will I be finding the owner?'

'Ye're no' seriously thinking . . . ?' began his engineman in alarm, but the Skipper shook free of his warning grasp.

'Where will I be finding the owner?'

The landlord, who was a kind-hearted man, said as he picked up the Skipper's glass, 'I wouldn't take them too seriously, Captain MacTaggart. I think maybe they're pulling your leg.'

'Pulling my leg!' The Skipper glowered as laughter shattered the pretence. At a dozen tables men were leaning back, eyes closed in enjoyment of the tremendous joke. 'As if you could get a cargo . . . !' 'Have to sell the old tub for scrap.'

Skipper and engineman stood side by side with their backs against the counter. 'There's not a word of truth in it!' McGregor protested. 'We've got plenty of work!'

The Skipper nodded. 'A very important cargo waiting for us in Campbeltown. But I just thought, as we were here, I'd ask if there wasna somebody who . . .'

'In Glasgow?' the ferry pilot asked, doubled over his table with laughter.

'With the owner of the last cargo still looking for you to serve a warrant?'

'There's no need for us to be asking favours,' the Skipper said with dignity. 'We're still greatly respected in the trade.'

'Ach, if ye rebuilt the *Maggie* from hawse-holes to stern-post they might let ye sail on Queen's Park boating pond!'

The Skipper picked up a glass from the counter and drained it before the engineman could see what was happening. Then he turned on his grinning tormentors with passion. 'Pach! Ye're very smug wi' your bonny caps and your five-days-a-week and your pensions and all! But ye're no better than hirelings, standing like wee bairns in front of Mr Campbell's big desk down there! Ye hav'na the freedom of operations that I have! Ye hav'na the dignity of your own command!'

From the corner of his eye he saw the swing door open and shut. His wary brain registered the fact and no more.

'. . . And as for my boat, there's no' a finer vessel in the coastal trade, no' a finer vessel anywhere! There's . . .' He stopped apprehensively as the wee boy came pushing between the tables.

'There's two men aboard us! In bowler hats!'

The Skipper gaped at the engineman. 'Inspectors!'

Like sprinters off the mark they started for the door. Then, remembering, stopped together by a cubicle. 'Hamish!'

As the mate came out with tousled hair and brick-red face to a fresh roar of laughter the landlord remembered the Skipper's drink. 'Here! That'll be sevenpence!'

McGregor and Hamish rushed into the street as the Skipper fumbled in his pockets and catechised the boy. 'Ye didna tell them ower much?'

'I said ye're awa' at Pollockshaws for your mither's funeral and ye'll no' be back for a fortnight.'

'What did they say to that?'

'They said they'd wait.'

The Skipper gave up the vain search, as he heard the mate's impatient call from outside. He said to the boy, 'I've no change. Pay him, will ye lad?' and a gust of laughter followed him into the street.

The boy moved indignantly through the grinning faces to the bar, where he counted slowly and carefully five pennies, three ha'pennies and two farthings.

'They were saying the truant officer's after ye, laddie, for going to sea before you'd finished the school,' Captain Jamieson baited.

The boy did not look up from his counting as he replied, 'It's a lie. I'm over fifteen.'

10

'Well, you'll be able to finish your schooling now. The *Maggie* will no' be putting out again.'

The boy looked at him fiercely. 'She *will*.'

'Ach, it's time Peter MacTaggart was put ashore, anyway. He's no' fit to be in charge of . . .' The big man did not finish the sentence as the boy dashed at him in passion.

'Ye'll no' say that about the Captain!'

Caught off balance Jamieson was knocked from his stool. For a moment there was general confusion – laughter, shouts of encouragement, threats – until the landlord grabbed the boy's collar. 'Come away, now! You've no business in a pub, anyway . . .'

As the boy was dragged outside the men in the bar leaned over their drinks and laughed like an audience at the end of a good comedy. They were sorry it was over. In a few minutes the landlord came back grinning. 'The wee divil!'

He ducked as a large turnip struck him on the shoulder and smashed against the wall with a glorious mess, breaking a couple of glasses. 'The wee divil!'

Chapter Three

In spite of a natural reluctance to meet the inspectors the boy was drawn irresistibly down the cobbled hill towards the *Maggie*. He came with dragging steps across the dock and stood beside the mate. Below, like the figures of a tragedy, the Skipper and McGregor were listening to the two inspectors. From the dock their conversation was inaudible, but the Skipper's drooping line as he touched, almost caressed, the wood of the boat was unmistakable. The boy looked up at the mate.

He asked, 'Is it the loading licence?'

'Aye.'

'If they take it away, we'll no' be able to carry any cargo at all.'

'Aye.'

'No' until she has her plates repaired?'

'Aye.'

'Is that what we need three hundred pounds for?'

'Aye, that's right.'

They stood back resentfully as the inspectors came up the wooden ladder.

'Could we no' borrow the money?' the boy asked miserably.

The mate looked down at him cynically. 'Who from?'

In his wheelhouse the Skipper looked out over the crowded water: smart steamers, cargo boats loading busily, the river patrol. A hooter called a challenge, and another answered from downstream. The huge cranes swung steadily to and fro. The river was alive with success.

The Skipper turned heavily towards the deck and climbed with McGregor up the ladder to the wharf. A seagull, momentarily disturbed, fluttered from the rail and perched disrespectfully a few yards away. Without speaking the Skipper started up the hill towards the town, and, like a funeral procession, his crew prepared to follow.

At first, as he climbed the hill and passed the pub, they could not even guess his intention. The boy thought that he must be wandering at random to wear out his depression, but the mate and the engineman, who had known him longer, guessed that some dark scheme was already turning in that agile brain. Crises were part of their daily life, and they had never seen the Skipper floored by one for long. But they were surprised when he stopped before the CSS offices.

They stood beside him looking through the plate-glass window at a neat model of a cargo vessel, framed photographs of impressive-looking ships, and beyond, to the reception hall and smart modern offices of the shipping company. They looked in wonder at a world so far removed from theirs that it was as incredible as any palace in an Arabian Night's tale. Behind them was the world they knew – rattling trams, errand boys, dock workers in dungarees: only a mile away their own *Maggie* lay, her rusted hulk on the oily waters of the Clyde. But here was wealth. They turned away, embarrassed, as a lady secretary eyed them severely.

In a sordid doorway they held an impromptu conference. The mate said, with a note of admiration, 'Ye're not going in there – to bait old Campbell?'

'Why not?' The Skipper was plainly not as confident as he would have liked to be. 'We can offer him a quarter share in the *Maggie* for three hundred pounds . . .'

McGregor asked, 'What about Sarah?'

'I could say my sister has a – a sort of *share* in the boat, but it's a family concern and I'm acting on her behalf.'

McGregor nodded doubtfully. 'Aye . . . aye . . . It's a gude idea.'

They moved with a brave show of confidence up the street and through the revolving doors into the reception hall, which was even larger and more luxuriously furnished than had appeared from the street. Some of the employees, smartly-dressed men and elegant young ladies, were just going to lunch. Two CSS officers, recognising the Skipper, grinned as they passed.

'Good morning.' The manager's secretary floated before them like a cool and efficient fairy. 'Can I help you?'

The Skipper said sturdily, 'We'd like to speak wi' Mr Campbell.'

She glanced towards a door marked 'MANAGER, Private' which only partly excluded the sound of voices raised in irritated argument. She said, 'Well, I'm afraid Mr

Campbell's engaged at the moment. And he's already late for a luncheon appointment. But if you'd care to wait . . .'

McGregor stepped forward aggressively. 'We canna afford to wait long. We've no time to waste.'

At this moment the manager's door opened, and Campbell, a middle-aged, humorous-looking Scot, came out of the office, carrying a hat and overcoat. He said to the secretary, 'Telephone and say I'm on my way . . .' He put on his coat and turned irritably back to the open doorway of his office.

'You've heard what Captain Jamieson says, Mr Pusey. His ship won't be ready before tomorrow night. We've no other vessel available.'

'Mr Campbell, if you'll wait just one moment: I'm getting through now.' Pusey, who was standing by the desk with the telephone in one hand, was a well-dressed, humourless, extremely nervous Englishman. At his elbow Captain Jamieson watched with stolid patience. Pusey complained petulantly, 'Mr Marshall's not going to like this. Mr Marshall can be a very impatient man . . .'

'Impatient or not,' Campbell said, 'I'm afraid . . .' He beckoned to Captain Jamieson. 'See if you can get me a taxi.'

As Jamieson crossed the reception hall he looked curiously at the crew of the *Maggie* and grinned, but he had no time to talk. Pusey was shouting into the receiver, 'Hello! World International Airways? It's Mr Pusey here! Will you put me through to Mr Marshall, please. Yes, I'm phoning from Glasgow.' Campbell looked at his watch, shrugged his shoulders, and moved out into the reception hall. With his attention divided between Pusey and his luncheon appointment he hardly noticed the Skipper, who had come cautiously to his elbow.

'Mr Campbell, if ye could spare us a moment.'

Campbell looked at him distractedly and then away again as Pusey shouted: 'Yes, I'll hold on.' Pusey put his hand over the mouthpiece and turned to Campbell. 'The cargo should have gone to Kiltarra days ago. Mr Marshall has two architects and any number of builders waiting. I'm sure Mr Marshall would pay the highest rates if the Captain could see his way to . . .' He held the telephone to attention. 'Mr Marshall? Pusey here, sir.'

As Campbell hesitated in irritation, the Skipper, prompted by a gesture from McGregor, cleared his throat. 'Mr Campbell, sir . . .'

Pusey was saying, 'No, it hasn't. Well, there's been a further delay, Mr Marshall. It's the shipping agency. They say . . .'

'Mr Campbell, sir, there's a matter of business we'd like to discuss wi' ye. If ye can spare . . .'

Campbell gave a harassed smile. 'I'm sorry, MacTaggart. I simply haven't the time. If you'll come back this afternoon after three.'

Inside the office Pusey was complaining, 'But I've tried *everything*, Mr Marshall . . . There simply isn't a boat of *any* description available for charter . . .'

Campbell raised his hands in a gesture of resignation and hurried out to the waiting taxi.

For a moment the Skipper was nonplussed. He didn't want to lose Campbell, but his canny Scots brain had already registered the nervous Pusey as a lamb. McGregor had come to the same assessment, and the Skipper found himself being urged across into Campbell's office, where the Englishman was still plaintively bleating, 'Not before tomorrow night, sir, and even then they can't guarantee . . . I know, Mr Marshall, but there just *isn't* a *boat* . . .'

The Skipper said in a matter-of-fact voice, 'If it's a cargo for Kiltarra ye have . . .'

Pusey looked up, startled. 'What?'

'There's a boat right here.'

For a moment, as Pusey turned wildly from the telephone, the fate of the *Maggie* trembled in the balance. The Skipper, concealing his nervousness behind a façade of indifference, looked at the pictures on the wall – the portrait of a past president, a handsome boat, pride of the CSS Line. The office clock beat out the systole and diastole of chance; an irate voice crackled from the receiver.

Pusey wailed, 'I'm sorry, Mr Marshall, only . . .' Stung to action he turned desperately on the Skipper. 'But I don't understand. Mr Campbell just this minute said . . .' He temporised into the mouthpiece. 'Excuse me, sir, there seems to be some confusion. Now they say there *is* a boat. But Mr Camp . . . Sir? The Captain?' He asked hoarsely, 'Are you the Captain?'

'Aye.'

'Yes, Mr Marshall. The . . . certainly, sir.' He handed the receiver to the Skipper, who accepted it with the caution of one who does not wholly believe in the telephone. Pusey muttered, 'It's Mr Marshall on the line. Calvin B. Marshall, General Overseas Manager of World International Airways.'

The Skipper spoke gruffly into the telephone. 'Aye. Aye! Captain MacTaggart speaking. Aye. Aye. We have.'

Pusey, who was now seeing him properly for the first time, had his first qualm of uneasiness, which was not lessened by the sight of the mate, the engineman and the boy looking expectantly through the open doorway.

The Skipper was saying, 'And ye want it to Kiltarra by Thursday noon. Oh, easily, easily. Insurance?' The very word seemed to impress him. 'Four thousand *pounds*! Aye, we'll see to it, sir. Aye. Who . . . ?' With relief he handed the telephone back to Pusey and winked solemnly to McGregor outside.

'Mr Marshall, I'm still not quite sure . . .' Pusey began, trying to voice his uneasiness, but he was frozen into obedience by the crackle of authority. 'Well . . . yes, Mr Marshall. I will, sir. Yes, Mr Marshall. Goodbye, Mr . . .' Miserably he replaced the receiver.

As he looked up and saw the Skipper standing respectfully by the table and the two men and a boy who had moved guilelessly into the room, he had an absurd feeling that he was trapped. There was no one in the reception hall outside. The office was empty. A lamb must feel like this surrounded by determined but not-too-hungry wolves. To quell his apprehension he turned vigorously to the Skipper. 'Will you tell me why, if a boat is available, Mr Campbell didn't *say* so? He placed me in a most embarrassing position!'

The Skipper said, 'We were just trying to explain to him, sir . . .'

As Pusey moved nervously across the room to the overcoat he had left on a chair he was aware that the crew were moving into new positions. The boy was hovering by Campbell's desk, examining the objects with interest: the inkwell, a paper-weight, a fountain pen: the inkwell, a paper-weight . . . Pusey felt that he must get out into the free air. He could have sworn there had been a fountain pen.

He asked, 'Where is your boat lying?'

The Skipper jerked his thumb. 'No' far from here. Just down the road.'

'Well, if you don't mind, I'll just have a look at it. 'Make sure it's a sound boat,' Mr Marshall said. 'That's all that matters.' Pusey put on his Homburg hat, picked up his briefcase, and went innocently into the cruel world.

Chapter Four

Along the busy street and down the steep cobbled hill the Skipper and McGregor had difficult in keeping pace with the Englishman. Not only was he in a hurry, but he couldn't suppress a feeling that the worst was still to come. They didn't *look* respectable. He walked quickly, with short mincing steps, and the Skipper and McGregor, who were the brains of the *Maggie*, kept doggedly at his shoulder. They left Hamish and the boy trailing behind.

As they came out on to the open wharf Pusey hesitated, blinking in the sunlight. 'Where is the . . . ?'

The Skipper gave a vague motion. 'This way, sir.'

Pusey could see only one vessel in that direction. To a landsman it looked substantial enough, and as he walked across the rough concrete of the wharf he felt relieved that his fears should have been proved unfounded. With more warmth than he he had dared to show before he asked, 'Now, will you give me an estimate of the charges?'

The Skipper hedged. 'Well, it's difficult to say exactly, sir . . .' then, catching the engineman's signal – three fingers held aloft – 'maybe . . . perhaps . . . three hundred pounds . . .'

Pusey stopped. 'That does seem rather high. However . . .' He fumbled with his briefcase. 'The goods are lying at Berth 17, Customs House Dock, checked and crated ready for shipment. Mainly plumbing and heating apparatus, some timber – a variety of materials, all extremely valuable.'

The Skipper tried to look impressed. 'Aye.'

'So,' Pusey said, 'I've been instructed to make sure that the ship is perfectly sound.'

The Skipper nodded uneasily. He hung back a few steps, wanting the engineman's support. This, they knew, was where fortune could desert them. Following reluctantly across the wharf they were surprised to see the direction Pusey was taking. Ignoring the *Maggie* he seemed to be making for the big cargo ship alongside. It was a minute before they realised that from his position on the wharf only the top of the *Maggie's* derrick was showing. The Skipper called half-heartedly, 'Er . . . Mr . . . er . . .' but Pusey was too far away to hear. The Skipper had the grace to feel embarrassed.

Urged on by McGregor and followed by Hamish and the boy, he approached the lower end of the gangplank and looked up to where Pusey was surveying the cargo ship. Far below, the *Maggie* rubbed against the dock.

Pusey called down. 'Ah, yes, well, I see no cause for concern on that score.' He seemed to be gaining reassurance every minute. As he came down the gangplank he asked, 'Shall we return to the office? Or,' glancing at his watch, 'better still, if we could settle the matter here . . .'

'Aye,' said McGregor with enthusiasm. 'That's a better idea.'

The Skipper was in a state of tension. Up on the cargo ship an officer, strolling along the deck, paused curiously to watch the little group of strangers on his gangplank.

Pusey was saying. 'I think, in the circumstances, I can – uh – agree to the – uh – three hundred. If you'll just sign the inventory. In triplicate, please.' He took a folder from his briefcase, spread out three typed lists, and handed the Skipper a pen.

Against the deck rail Nemesis leant and watched while the Skipper weighed up the chances – solvency or jail. 'Where do I sign?'

Pusey said, 'Mr Marshall spoke to you about the insurance. I take it I can leave that to you?'

McGregor agreed heartily, 'Och aye. Just leave it to us.'

'Yes, well . . .' Although he couldn't have explained why, Pusey felt his doubts returning. A fine ship, newly painted, obviously seaworthy. . . . They only had to go to Kiltarra. But he said, 'Just one thing: I'd like Mr Campbell to ring me at my office tomorrow morning, so that I can be certain everything got away all right.'

McGregor held the fort while the Skipper struggled with three signatures. 'Everything will get away all right. Aye.'

Pusey said nervously, 'Well, you'll want something on account, I presume.' He felt in his pocket. 'I'll give you a cheque for . . .'

The Skipper stood up, holding the pen and the three sheets of paper. Now that he was committed he had no regrets. 'Cash would be better, if ye can manage it,' he said.

'But I only have about fifty pounds . . .'

The Skipper held out his hand. 'That'll do fine, sir. You can let us have the rest when we've got the job done.'

'Well . . .' Pusey reluctantly passed over a wad of five-pound notes. He too was committed now and he wanted to get away. 'I'm afraid I must . . .' He held out his hand. 'Good morning.'

'And good day to ye, sir.'

Pusey hurried across the dock, trying to forget their excited faces and the boy raising his cap so respectfully. 'And gude luck to ye.'

With the money firmly in his hands the Skipper could afford to have a conscience. He said regretfully, 'It seems to me yon laddie's the victim of a serious misunderstanding.'

The mate came forward loyally. 'Ye didna tell him a thing that wasna true.'

But it was McGregor who solved all their doubts. He said happily, 'Ach, ye wouldna want him to deal with the CSS, would you? The villains would only try to do him down!'

Chapter Five

The door of the pub opened suddenly, and the *Maggie's* crew came roaring into the night. The Skipper and McGregor clung together in song; the mate was playing his concertina. Only the wee boy was entirely sober.

> 'I belong to Gleska
> Dear old Gleska toon . . .'

The road to the dock was steeper and more cluttered with obstacles than they remembered. Across the water, lights flickered entrancingly and multiplied to a glitter of diamonds. A ship's hooter was a brave sound that deserved a cheer. Lamp-posts leant tantalisingly from the touch, and in a sheltered doorway a policeman stood watching with clicking disapproval.

'I belong to Gleska . . .' They marched in line astern across the dock with the boy in front treading carefully through the darkness, the Skipper, the engineman, ready to fight the world, and Hamish, the mate, with his concertina.

'Careful now.' The boy had found the wooden ladder.

'I'm ower young to marry yet . . .' The Skipper halted as near the edge as the boy would permit, and sang with gusto to the night. Tears of happiness and emotion were in his eyes. He was still humming as he came down to the deck and went groping towards his cabin. He stopped by the hatch and looked back, puzzled. 'Who put my light on?'

McGregor and the boy were concentrating too much on their own course to answer any irrelevant questions and presently they heard the Skipper clumping down to his cabin. Then all peace was shattered.

A female voice cried fiercely, 'Ha! Ye thought I wouldna catch ye, ye scoundrel.'

'Sarah!' The Skipper's anguished cry pierced the stillness.

'But I've had people watching for ye *everywhere*,' the woman said.

Above, the engineman grasped the hatch. 'Holy smoke, it's Sarah!' He took a few cautious steps down into the cabin – enough to see Sarah MacTaggart standing menacingly above her brother. She was a large, badly-dressed, fearsome woman of fifty-five or so, and legally she could control the *Maggie*.

'Ye'll no' get away with it this time like the others,' Sarah was saying.

The Skipper was spectacularly upset. 'Sarah! I was comin' to see ye, Sarah . . .'

'Ye were nothing of the sort!'

'Will ye no' sit down, Sarah? And we can discuss . . .'

'There's nothing to discuss, ye black-hearted swindler! Ye owe me over four hundred pounds. And ye signed a paper what says I own the major share in the vessel!' She hit the bulkhead and looked with contempt at the dirt on her glove. 'The filthy thing! Well, she's no' worth a penny afloat but she'll fetch five hundred as scrap, and I'm going to *sell* her to get back my money.'

The mate and the engineman and the wee boy, who were listening at the lighted cowling above the Skipper's cabin, groaned dismally. McGregor said, 'She's got a court order! I told him not to put into Gleska, the old goat! He wouldn't . . .'

'He's *no*' an old goat,' the boy said, bridling.

'Oh, shut your blethering!'

In the cabin the Skipper seemed stunned by his sister's ruthlessness. He nodded slowly, then turned away and took a bottle of whisky and two glasses from the locker. He said heavily, 'Aye. Aye. I'm glad ye've come, Sarah. I'll no' be giving ye an argument. The *Maggie's* yours.'

'And what treachery are ye scheming now?' She shied away from the whisky. 'I'll no' drink wi' ye. It wouldna surprise me if it was *drugged*.'

The Skipper shook his head sadly and proceeded to pour out two stiff measures. He said, with conscious pathos, 'Ye don't trust me, Sarah. Ach, ye're right. And ye're right to take the boat, for it's time I was giving it up. A man can only give so many years to the sea. The best man there is has to be put ashore at the end.' He put his hand dramatically on his heart. 'And I didna write to ye because I thought ye might worry yourself . . . but I've no' been well . . .'

Believing none of this, his sister suddenly swung her handbag at him striking his shoulder a solid blow. She said scornfully, 'You're as strong as a horse!'

'No, no.' The Skipper looked round at the familiar objects of his tiny cabin and nodded sadly. 'Aye. I was born aboard the *Maggie*, sixty years ago, and I'd always hoped – that one day I would die aboard her.'

For the first time Sarah felt uneasy. She eyed him reflectively as she sipped her whisky. 'There's no need to talk like that.'

'But we're both already overdue for the breaker's yard,' the Skipper said, topping up her glass. He turned away, apparently overcome by emotion, and covered his face with his hands.

Sarah protested doubtfully, 'Ye'll no' get round me like that, d'ye hear, Peter MacTaggart?'

In terrible despair the Skipper confessed, 'I said to myself, if only we could do this job, if only we could get this three hundred pounds, then ye might agree to wait for the rest. But I was afraid to come and see ye till I had the money to hand to ye.'

'Three hundred pounds?' asked Sarah, drinking quickly.

'Aye.' He shook his head. 'But ye might never get it. The *Maggie's* no' sound. If she sank on the way . . .'

'Ye'd never let her sink! Whatever's to be said against ye, you're a seaman like your father.'

'I'm an old man, Sarah.'

She poured herself another drink. 'Ach, will ye stop *talking* like that! What's the matter wi' ye? I may have been o'er-hasty . . . Let me think.'

On the open deck Hamish embraced McGregor, and McGregor embraced the boy. They were still talking and laughing quietly together a quarter of an hour later when the Skipper and his sister emerged from the cabin. McGregor, who was Sarah's sworn enemy, was profoundly affable, bowing, scraping, smiling, almost falling overboard, as she pushed her massive body through the hatch. She glared at him suspiciously and then turned to her brother, who was following her out of the hatch.

'But mind ye, it's me to handle the business.'

The Skipper touched her arm reassuringly. 'Of course, Sarah. It's right that ye should. I'll take ye to the CSS office in the morning. It was through them we got the cargo.'

She crossed the deck and wheezed up the first rungs of the ladder. Then she paused as a new suspicion threatened her peace of mind. 'How am I to know you won't sneak away before morning?'

'Sarah!' The Skipper was hurt. 'Besides, the tide is falling, we *couldna* get out before nine in the morning.'

She said firmly, 'I'll be here at eight.'

The crew watched with admiration and excitement as the Skipper climbed up beside Sarah on the dock. He said praisingly, 'Ye're nae so copious aboot the body as when I last saw ye. It becomes ye.'

She turned away, pleased. 'Och, ye old flatterer!'

The Skipper took a pace forward and kissed her on the cheek. He said, 'I canna tell ye what it means to me having your encouragement. It strengthens me, Sarah.'

She called, sentimentally, 'Good night.'

'Good night to ye, Sarah.'

As she turned, a few paces away, she saw him standing alone, an old, tired, almost broken but not quite defeated man who was determined somehow to carry on. Warmed by emotion and the unaccustomed whisky she climbed slowly up the hill.

As soon as she had disappeared into the darkness the Skipper became a changed man. He skipped down the ladder like a mountain goat and called in a hoarse whisper, 'Get ready to get under way! The sooner we're out of here the better. Ach, the auld battle-axe!'

The crew accepted the emergency. McGregor slid down to his engine-room, Hamish loosened the ropes on the bollards. It was not long before the *Maggie* was chugging quietly away from the dock: its dark, unexpected shape pushed out into the river and the ripples of its wake spread across the quiet waters. Only the boy seemed unhappy. For a moment he stood near the bow, watching the black mirror of water. Then, turning, he walked up to join the others – the mate coiling a rope, the engineman at his hatch, the Skipper leaning from the window of his wheelhouse.

The boy called, 'Captain, sir?' He voiced his doubts with deference. 'What you said about the tide, sir . . . Is that no' true? Are we no' a bit late trying to get down this way?'

They turned on him with a unanimity that suggested they secretly held the same doubts.

'Haud your whisht! What do you know about it?'

'Ye're no' the Captain yet, laddie.'

'Ye're getting over-cheeky. Get forrard and make us some tea!'

Crestfallen, the boy went back towards the fo'c'sle hatch in the bows, but he had still some yards to go when he was flung violently off his feet. With a scraping noise and a violent shudder the ship ground to a standstill.

Chapter Six

(1)

Calvin B. Marshall, General Overseas Manager of World International Airways, was a man dedicated to efficiency. Time was more to him than money. Telephones, dictaphones, electric buzzers, loudspeakers, teleprinters: these were the weapons with which he fought against the erosion of precious hours and minutes. From early morning until late evening his office bustled with swift, efficient movement and the hubbub of urgent conversation. The telephone was a fractious master whose impatient ring must be instantly answered.

In such a kingdom Pusey was a lord high chamberlain. He would do, or try to do, anything that was ordered. As he came with a worried frown from the manager's room Marshall's voice sounded angrily through the outer office: '. . . know as well as I do that we can't afford mistakes. The first principle of sound business administration . . .' Pusey closed the door, leaving the three departmental managers to their fate.

'Mr Campbell's on the line now, Mr Pusey.' Miss Peters, Marshall's smart young secretary, held out the telephone.

'Thank you.' He came fussily across, but as he lifted the receiver to his ear it was plain that his attention was still on the glazed door where Marshall's shadow, the forceful gesticulating hand, could be seen.

'Hello! Mr Campbell?' He heard the broad Scottish acknowledgment four hundred miles away in Glasgow. 'Mr Campbell, I was rather anxious, so I thought I'd call *you*. I trust the cargo got away all right.'

'What cargo would that be?'

'Why the cargo on the boat, of course.'

'What boat?'

'What boat! The boat I chartered yesterday!' He tried to keep calm, but the seed of panic was there in his brain. Miss Peters, standing efficiently at his side, looked at him enquiringly, ready with pencil and notebook, a directory, another telephone. Marshall's voice still boomed terror through the door.

In Glasgow Campbell was saying, 'You found a boat, then? Well done!'

'Found a boat!' Pusey put one hand over the mouthpiece as he turned to Miss Peters. 'Really, this man is *utterly impossible*!' Into the telephone he said, 'Surely you've *heard* from your Captain MacTaggart.'

Campbell was saying, 'This laddie's off his head,' only he didn't trouble to cover the mouthpiece. He said, 'D'ye mean to say ye made arrangements with MacTaggart?'

Pusey was covering his eyes with his free hand. 'Really,

Mr Campbell, in all my experience . . .' His whole body stiffened with feminine indignation as laughter came echoing from the receiver. 'I'm so glad you find it humorous!'

The voice on the telephone spluttered an apology. 'I'm sorry, Mr Pusey. Only Captain Jamieson here heard me use MacTaggart's name. He was telling me about all the fuss down at Broomilaw.'

'Fuss? Broomilaw? Do you think you could possibly explain?'

'Yes, well . . .' There was a moment of indistinct talk as though Captain Jamieson was finishing the story, and then Campbell bellowed again with laughter. 'Ye mean it's still there?'

Pusey pursed his lips and waited.

At last, as the laughter died down, Campbell came back on the line. 'Mr Pusey, I really must apologise. Only, I must tell you – MacTaggart has nothing to do with our organisation. He's master of an old Puffer – aye, the *Maggie*. And d'ye mean to say ye put your cargo on his boat?' He began to laugh again. 'Ach, the chances are ye've seen the last of it! But I can give ye a piece of information about it. Something I've just heard. Early this morning . . .'

As he recounted with gusto the truth about MacTaggart and about the *Maggie* and her crew poor Pusey listened with growing horror. His eyes widened. Beads of sweat appeared on his forehead. 'Oh, no . . . Oh, no . . . but that isn't possible!' Adding to his horror the door of Marshall's room opened and the three executives came out, self-consciously, like schoolboys who had felt the cane. Pusey's wild stare followed them across the office, then back again as the intercommunication set on Miss Peters' desk clicked to authority. 'Send Pusey in.'

The sound of his master's voice seemed to fill Pusey with almost animal terror. His lips trembled. His eyes bulged. Blindly putting the receiver down on Miss Peters' desk he stumbled across the room towards Marshall's office, and Campbell's laughter followed him like a banshee call from another world.

On first sight Calvin B. Marshall was the man that Pusey had always imagined him to be – fierce, cruel, utterly ruthless, yet on watching him dispassionately you could see from the eyes and the sudden unexpected quirk to the mouth that he was a man of humour, possibly even kindliness. He waited at his desk impatiently – for he had just given a justifiable rebuke to three senior executives – and to Pusey he seemed like a Grand Inquisitor ready to begin the torture. On the mahogany top of his desk lay the evidence of his authority – a welter of papers, graphs and charts, some silver-plated trophies, including a model of a four-engined World International Airways aircraft. There was also a large leather frame holding a photograph of his wife.

In a querulous voice Pusey began his tale of woe. He was so near to tears that Marshall had difficulty in understanding exactly what had happened.

'. . . and he gave me his signature!' Pusey cried.

'Well?'

'He signed the inventory.'

'So?'

'So naturally I – I chartered the boat.'

'And?'

Pusey burst out, with rising hysteria, 'They weren't who they said they were. And Campbell says the cargo's *not* on the boat, it's in Glasgow, and the man I spoke to – he hasn't a boat at all, but something called a Puffer! And instead of being well on its way to Kiltarra it was stuck on the subway, and not even the right boat . . .'

'Just a moment!' Calvin B. Marshall was quite calm, but he was looking as though he feared for Pusey's sanity. 'Just let me get one thing straight. You say . . . a boat is stuck on the subway?'

(2)

It was. The *Maggie* was perched about fifty yards from the north bank of the Clyde with her bows down and her stern ludicrously propped up, well out of the water. Her propeller was showing, and the dinghy, which was attached by a painter, was hanging vertically from the stern. A police boat was lying alongside, and another boat, with three figures in it, was going out from the bank. On the bridge and along the embankment a growing crowd of Glaswegians enjoyed the spectacle and encouraged the crew of the *Maggie* with ribald witticisms.

Sitting despondently in the engine-room hatchway McGregor ignored their taunts. Beside him the mate lay stretched out on the deck, asleep. Only the boy gave moral support to the Skipper, who was leaning from his wheel-house to continue his argument with a policeman.

'You'd no right to put out at that state of the tide!' the policeman was saying as he climbed, discomfited, into his patrol boat. 'You may have damaged the . . .'

'And what about the damage to my ship!' the Skipper demanded indignantly.

As the patrol boat moved gently in the swell, a rowboat pulled steadily across the oily water towards the *Maggie*. There were three men aboard, the owner, pulling laconically at the oars as though, having passed his life with seafaring men, he had lost the capacity for surprise, and two pressmen who were looking towards a story with incredulous delight. As the owner shipped his oars, the photographer took his camera from its case and squinted up at the *Maggie*. The reporter stood up and hailed the Skipper.

'Captain MacTaggart, I'm from the *Star*. Would you care to make a statement?'

For the benefit of the policemen the Skipper shouted, 'Ye can say I'm considering bringing an action.'

The reporter grinned. 'Good for you, Captain! What's your destination?'

'Kiltarra.'

The policemen, deciding regretfully that there was nothing to be done, sailed upstream, their launch cutting neat ripples through the water. Taking this as a moral victory for the *Maggie* the onlookers raised a cheer.

'What are you carrying?' the reporter called.

The Skipper, hanging out of the wheelhouse, raised his voice so that it would carry to the scoffers on the bank. 'A very valuable cargo what belongs to Mr Calvin B. Marshall, of World International Airways . . .'

'Are you now?' Visibly impressed, the reporter made a note. 'And you're going to Kiltarra, Captain?'

'Aye.'

'As soon as you're – afloat?'

'Aye.'

'How do you propose to get her off, Captain?'

'How d'ye think? I'll wait for the tide.'

Along the bank and the bridge the audience, growing restless, continued their catcalls. 'Ahoy! Captain Carlsen! Are ye hanging on?' The Skipper and his crew bristled with indignation as they waited for the tide.

Chapter Seven

One reason for Calvin B. Marshall's success was that when things went wrong he was not afraid of making himself responsible for putting them right. Within an hour of hearing Pusey's miserable story he was on a plane bound for Glasgow.

It was a BEA plane – belonging to their chief rivals – but even he, the General Overseas Manager of World International Airways, could find nothing to criticise. They had left Northolt punctual to the minute, and now reclining in a deeply cushioned seat, with the green map of England rolling pleasantly below, he could feel for the first time a certain satisfaction in this small adventure. For the moment he was relaxed. In the next seat – a silk stocking, a neat shoe, the open notebook on her knee – sat the efficient Miss Peters. Across the gangway Pusey sat and perspired.

Mr Marshall felt sorry for Pusey. So far as he could tell from his garbled story, this unscrupulous Skipper MacTaggart had tricked him into sending the cargo – Marshall's cargo – by some wretched little boat called a

Puffer. Mercifully, the boat had run aground before it had cleared Glasgow docks. Marshall, who could always admire initiative, looked forward to meeting MacTaggart. He bore him no grudge. A short flight to Glasgow, an hour there to settle the matter: he could be back in London in the morning. He remembered that tomorrow evening his wife was giving a dinner party.

He must have dozed then, for when he opened his eyes the plane was stationary on the tarmac and Pusey was touching him deferentially on the arm. 'If you're ready, sir. I've hired a car.'

They drove to the centre of Glasgow. The commissionaire of the Central Hotel touched his hat as he opened the door. Pusey and Miss Peters fluttered round two porters who were carrying the bags. Speed and efficiency. Marshall dropped two coppers to a newsvendor standing at the kerb.

'Puffer aground on subway – "Will sue" says Skipper.' Below the caption, an ancient boat, ludicrously upended, held the centre of the page. Marshall smiled as he followed the porters to his suite.

In a few minutes – for he would waste no time even on an adventure – he had washed and was ready to tackle all the shipping companies and skippers in Glasgow. He called Pusey. 'Get this man Campbell on the phone. We'll start with him.'

'Certainly, sir.' Before Pusey could fumble through a directory, Miss Peters had handed him a slip with the telephone number of the CSS offices. Campbell was in and ready to take the call.

'Ye're in Glasgow, Mr Pusey? Well, I must hand it to ye for quick work.' A chuckle; then, 'Have you seen the *Star*?'

'The *Star*?'

'It's our newspaper. There's a picture in it would interest you. The puffer *Maggie* – the boat your cargo's on.'

While Pusey was listening to this, Marshall, following the trend of conversation, had pushed the front page of the *Star* before him. Pusey had time to read the headline and gain an impression of the photograph. 'Very humorous, Mr Campbell, I'm sure!'

'No offence, Mr Pusey. I'm glad ye decided to come. There's two people here would like to see ye.'

'Indeed!'

'Aye. There's a reporter called Fraser, from the *Star*, and there's a good lady who says she owns the *Maggie*.'

'Really! Well, I must say that, considering it was your fault that this fraud was perpetrated in the first place, I think it's your duty to come here.'

Campbell said with just a hint of Scottish granite, 'Well, I don't know if I like your tone, Mr Pusey.'

'I'm sorry about that.'

'I don't think I understand you when you say that the CSS bears any responsibility in the matter.'

'Surely it's clear enough.'

'And another thing,' Campbell said, recovering his sense of humour, 'when you were in my office the other day, did you by any chance take my fountain pen?'

'Really, Mr Campbell, I . . .'

'Here, let me speak to him.' Marshall took the phone before any more valuable minutes could be wasted. He said pleasantly, 'Mr Campbell? Calvin B. Marshall speaking. I'm sorry to trouble you. We seem to be causing you quite a bit of bother . . . Yes, I've just come up to get things straightened out . . . Yes, at the Central. I'd be very much obliged if you could manage to spare me a few minutes . . . Here? That's very kind of you. Thank you, Mr Campbell.'

Pusey, watching him replace the receiver, was both indignant and defensive. 'Well, I mean to say, if you're in a man's office and other people come into it and begin discussing the same subjects with you, surely it's reasonable to assume . . .'

Marshall patted his arm. 'Take it easy, Pusey. There's no need to get into a panic. It won't help matters to try to blame this man Campbell for your mistakes.'

'Well, if I may say so, Mr Marshall, I think the fact that *you* spoke to Captain MacTaggart yourself . . .'

Marshall accepted the point. 'All right, Pusey. It doesn't matter who's to blame. I'll have it sorted out in an hour. You'd better book sleepers for us on the night train to London.'

Still offended, Pusey took up the telephone. 'Hello, operator.' He said indignantly to Miss Peters, 'He even had the effrontery to ask if I'd taken his fountain pen!'

Pusey's indignation had a chance to smoulder in the next half-hour. Although the CSS offices were not a great distance from the Central, Campbell was not a man to waste shillings on taxis unless speed was essential, and now, enjoying the thought of all the trouble MacTaggart had caused, he preferred to walk. It was therefore with the greatest good humour that he knocked at the door of

Marshall's suite, only to be met by a severely businesslike Miss Peters, with Pusey glowering in the background.

'Ah, Mr Campbell. So there you are at last!'

'Good evening, Mr Pusey.' Campbell felt rather than saw the figures in the corridor and turning, bewildered, he saw that Fraser, the reporter, and Sarah MacTaggart had followed him grimly through the streets. He made a shrugging gesture, disowning responsibility, and explained, 'There's a reporter from the *Star* and a . . .'

'If you'll step this way,' Pusey interrupted pompously, and led the way into the inner room – Marshall's room. The door was opened and closed too quickly for him to realise that Miss Peters was at that moment being brushed aside by two people who could make the difficult situation practically impossible.

In the inner room Marshall was standing by the window with the *Star*. He still found the adventure almost incredible and he looked up with amusement as Pusey entered.

Pusey waved an introduction. 'Mr Campbell, Mr Marshall.'

For a moment the two men eyed each other warily but with respect. Then Marshall held out his hand. 'How do you do, Mr Campbell? It's very kind of you to give us your help in this matter.'

'Not at all, Mr Marshall.'

'Sit down, won't you? Can I offer you a drink?'

'I'll have a whisky, thank you.'

Marshall gestured to Pusey. 'And a Vichy water for me.' He picked up the newspaper again and showed it to Campbell. 'Quite a boat. Is that MacTaggart?'

Campbell made no attempt to hide his smile. 'Aye.'

Pusey, who was telephoning for the drinks, could not see how anyone could find this disgraceful episode funny. His fingers drummed nervously, the brow was furrowed with responsibility. 'Room service?'

He knew when Miss Peters came fluttering into the room that you could never be sure that there were not new trials and irritations to meet. She tripped across to him and whispered, 'Mr Pusey, if you could spare a minute . . .' It was the first time he had seen Miss Peters scared.

He followed her irritably outside and was startled by what he saw. Standing with feet astride and arms akimbo, Sarah looked like some vengeful goddess; Kali, perhaps, dressed – but not too well dressed – in western garments. In the background, and obviously enjoying the situation, was the reporter, Fraser.

Pusey's nostrils quivered with disapproval. 'Miss Peters, who are these people?'

'People, indeed! I'll "people" you, young man,' said Sarah coming menacingly forward, with bag swinging.

'Really, madam, I only asked . . .' said Pusey, backing away in alarm.

'Then if that's the way ye ask I'll have to learn ye some manners.'

'No, no. I'm sorry.'

She paused, undecided, as though she would still dearly love to swing her bag at him, despite his apology.

With a trembling voice Pusey turned to Fraser, 'And who – who are you please?'

The reporter grinned, 'My name's Fraser.'

42

'Fraser?'

'I'm a reporter on the *Star*.'

'A reporter! Was it you who wrote that . . . that . . .?'

Fraser nodded cheerfully. 'That's right.'

'Well, I think you can take it, Mr Fraser, that you are not welcome here, not welcome at all.'

'Does that go for me?' Sarah demanded menacingly.

'No, no. Indeed not, madam. I was just going to ask . . .'

'What I'm here for? Well, I'll tell ye. Ye've concocted some scheme with that blackguard brither of mine, Peter MacTaggart.'

'No, madam, I assure you . . .'

She said fiercely. 'This Puffer you hired to go . . .'

'We *didn't* hire a Puffer . . .'

'It says in the paper you did! Are your goods aboard it or not?'

'Yes, but they won't be for long.'

Their attention wavered towards a waiter who had come in, with silver tray carrying whisky and Vichy water. Directed by Miss Peters he made for the door of Marshall's room.

Sarah started indignantly as she followed the implication. She pushed past the outraged Pusey. 'Here, I'll no' be put off by any underlings. I want to see the owner.'

'Please, madam . . . Please!'

'Out of my way, young man, 'less ye want a clout.'

'But please, madam. If you could just wait one moment.' Pusey danced before her like a fencing master, anguished, outraged, but determined that she should not pass.

Meanwhile in the inner room Marshall was beginning

to feel uneasy. He watched the waiter hand Campbell a glass of whisky but he refused his own Vichy water. He looked out over the street and then, as the waiter left, turned anxiously back to Campbell.

He said, 'Well, I don't want to go to the police, but I can tell you right now that from the look of her,' he slapped his hand against the newspaper, 'and the way this character MacTaggart navigates, I want my cargo off that boat. If your boat is available from tomorrow morning, let's radio MacTaggart to put into the nearest . . .'

Campbell shook his head. 'Ye canna do that. They've no radio.'

'But whoever heard of a cargo vessel without radio?'

Campbell said gently, 'You understand, they usually carry coal or . . .'

Marshall put his hands to his eyes. 'Coal! And I've got four thousand pounds' worth of stuff aboard it, that's taken me months to get together.' He sat down on the table, determined to remain calm. 'How *do* I get in touch with them?'

Campbell said, 'I can give ye a list of harbour and pier masters and their telephone numbers.'

Marshall jumped up with enthusiasm and made for the door. 'That's fine. I'll have Pusey start on it right . . .'

His voice trailed off as he opened the door and saw the wretched Pusey defending himself from Sarah. 'What the heck!'

Red-faced and malevolent, Sarah switched her attack to him. 'Ah, here ye are, then! And is that the kind of man ye are, to do a helpless old woman out o' her rights?'

'I beg your pardon, madam?' he said. 'All right, Pusey, let's go into my room and find out what this is all about.'

As he turned masterfully he caught an impression of Campbell's smile, then he was borne forward by the urgent tide of plaintiffs.

Pusey: 'Really, madam, I must insist. I – I'm sorry, Mr Marshall . . .'

Miss Peters: 'This lady says she is . . .'

Sarah: 'Don't you dare to touch me, young man. I'll have you know I'm the rightful owner of the . . .'

Marshall held up his hands. 'Here, just a minute.' He squared his shoulders and spoke in his Overseas Manager's voice. '*Please*! What is all this? Who is this lady?'

In the momentary silence Sarah pushed herself before him. She said with emphasis, 'Sarah MacTaggart, the legitimate owner of the Puffer, and I'm here to tell ye that whatever money it is that ye owe, it's to be paid to *me*, or I'll go to the police.'

Marshall said, in a reasonable tone, 'Well, Mrs MacTaggart . . .'

'Miss!'

'Well, Miss MacTaggart, I'm sorry to have to inform you that I don't owe any money at all. On the contrary! Your father, by resorting to tactics . . .'

'He's no' my father, he's my brither, the black-hearted . . .'

Marshall held on to the table. He said with a slow, measured calmness, 'Whoever he is, he practically stole four thousand pounds' worth of goods. By sheer misrepresentation . . .' He stopped, bewildered, as he saw another face in the nightmare, a young man standing behind this formidable female, a young man writing down all that was being said. Marshall pushed past Pusey and Miss Peters. He pointed wildly: 'Who – what – who is this . . . ?'

The young man said cheerfully, 'My name's Fraser, Mr Marshall. From the *Glasgow Star*.

It took a full minute for this to sink in. Then Marshall snatched the paper from the table. He shouted, 'What? Do you mean . . . ? Are you the one who thinks all this is so funny?'

It was a comparatively easy matter to get rid of the reporter, but it took all Miss Peters' diplomacy, all Marshall's determination, all Pusey's vicarious courage, to dispose of Sarah. At last as she was persuaded, foot by foot through the outer room and into the corridor, and as she departed with swinging bag and umbrella rampant towards the stairs she still continued to voice the most slanderous accusations against Marshall, the CSS, her brother, the unfortunate Pusey.

Marshall came back mopping his brow. Never had he felt less like a Napoleon of commerce. He needed encouragement. On the table was his glass of Vichy water and a whole bottle of whisky. He poured the Vichy water into a vase of flowers and topped up his glass with whisky.

As he lifted the glass and sipped gratefully he was aware of Campbell at the window, watching him with amusement. Campbell said, 'Ye'll no' be wanting to tackle that fearsome body again, Mr Marshall.'

Warmed by the whisky, Marshall nodded. 'If her brother's anything like that!'

From the window they watched Sarah emerge from the swing doors into the street. The commissionaire saluted deferentially, motioned with white glove towards a taxi, and received a buffet for his pains from Sarah's handbag.

'What a woman!'

Campbell sat at the table and wrote out a list from his pocket book. He said, 'Here's the list I was promising ye – all the harbour and pier masters. The *Maggie*'ll no' be so far.'

'Is she a fast boat?'

'Fast!' Campbell exploded. 'If McGregor, the engine-man, really sets his mind to it she'll do maybe three knots – four if they're really pushed.'

Marshall finished his whisky. 'And my cargo's on that!' He held out his hand. 'Well, Mr Campbell, I'm extremely grateful for your help in this matter. I'll get Pusey to phone these numbers straight away. It shouldn't be long before we contact MacTaggart, then I reckon everything will be under control.'

Campbell looked at him doubtfully, aware that Marshall still had little idea of the man he was up against, but remembering how much he had suffered already he thought it would be unkind to inform him of the suffering still to come.

When Campbell had gone Marshall settled down to work. Peace returned, and confidence. From his chair he could see, as he dictated to Miss Peters, the gaunt outline of the city: office buildings, dingy pubs, an arcade of shops. Beyond the roofs the factories rose, square and practical; tall chimneys, a haze of smoke, a crane moving like a finger above the docks. By altering the position of his chair a few inches he could look right down to the street where the office workers were flowing relentlessly along the pavements, across the roads, to be drawn, fifty, sixty at a time, on swaying trams. Factory workers passed on their way to a late shift. A few people, elderly women and courting couples, paid their shillings at the grille and went doubtfully into the lighted cinema down the road. Life was normal again.

'We should like to be sure of delivery . . .' With notebook open on her knee, pencil poised, the immaculate Miss Peters gently prompted.

'Sorry!' Marshall jerked back to his letter. 'We should like to be sure of delivery before the 27th instant.'

In the next room Pusey was working methodically down the list. 'Hallo, hallo. Greenock 61827? Is that the pier master?' Occasionally, like a warning rattle, the telephone bar would be irritably tapped. 'Hallo, miss. That was the wrong number you gave me. Well, I assure you! I asked plainly enough for . . .'

After dinner they returned to work. The hours lost in flying to Glasgow must be recovered somehow. Fortunately, by returning on the night sleeper, the journey back to London would cost them nothing in precious hours and minutes. A necessary extravagance was the telephone call from Marshall's wife.

He spoke to her quietly, almost deferentially, in a tone he used to no other person. 'That's right, honey, just a routine business matter . . . Uh-huh, either by train tonight or on the first plane tomorrow morning . . .'

As he spoke, Miss Peters came quickly into the room. She started to withdraw, but, as Marshall raised his finger, she remained. He saw that the strain of the day's business was beginning to show even on her usually untroubled brow. She stood fidgeting nervously until he finished.

'If I have to stay over, I'll ring you later tonight. . . . Yes, that's right. Well, thanks for calling, honey. Good night.'

He replaced the receiver, and turned with a smile of encouragement to Miss Peters. At least, this absurd episode had left no mark on *him*.

Miss Peters said, 'I've just had a call from the harbour master at Greenock, Mr Marshall. He says the Puffer arrived there ten minutes ago . . .'

Marshall nodded with satisfaction. 'Good. Now, here's the plan. First, tell Pusey to . . .'

Miss Peters interrupted him with hysteria in her voice, 'But, Mr Marshall, he said that when he gave them your instructions . . .' She faltered, seeing his expression.

'Yes?'

'Oh, Mr Marshall. They just sailed right out again!'

Chapter Eight

The *Maggie* steamed peacefully northwards through the blue waters of Loch Fyne. It was a perfect day. Along the shore the pleasant countryside, rolling hills, heathland, dark pine woods, showed clearly in the sunlight. A landward breeze flecked the water with white and filled the sails of passing yachts. Seagulls circled patiently over their wake and sometimes, wearying perhaps of the laggardly progress, came down to rest on the stern rail.

On deck the scene was as peaceful and untroubled as the day. McGregor was sitting on his hatch reading a comic book. Nearby the mate lay full-length in the sunshine as he struggled, not too successfully, with the intricacies of his concertina. Only the boy was working. He was scrubbing the deck – not because he had been told to do so, but because of his fierce inarticulate loyalty to the Skipper and the Skipper's boat.

From his wheelhouse the Skipper shouted down to McGregor, 'See if ye can't get another half-knot out of her. She's not making more than five.'

Without looking up from his comic McGregor answered, 'She's making six!'

'Five at the outside.'

'She's making six!'

The Skipper replied diplomatically, 'Then see if she'll do seven.'

McGregor rose slowly and came across the deck. 'She'll no' make seven, ye know that! What's the matter with ye? Considering that ye'll no' spend a penny to get her boilers cleaned . . .'

The Skipper said guardedly, 'Never mind about that. If we're to get to Kiltarra by . . .' He looked up, distracted by an aircraft that was diving down towards the loch. With the sun behind it and the cloudless sky it was difficult to see, and the Skipper turned to face McGregor, who was standing, full of argument, below his wheelhouse.

The engineman said, 'Who was it put the boat on the subway?'

'I'll have no insubordination aboard my vessel,' the Skipper threatened.

'Insubordination! Who was it who was too drunk to find the way out of Campbeltown harbour last . . . ?'

His voice was smothered by the roar of the engine as the aircraft, flying low over the water, swept a matter of yards, it seemed, above the deck. Startled by the suddenness the engineman almost jumped overboard. The boy looked up astounded. Even the mate jumped to his feet.

'What in the name of goodness!'

They stared as the plane banked and turned.

'It's coming back.'

They made for cover, the Skipper into his wheelhouse, McGregor into the engine-room, the mate flat on the deck. But the boy, with the courage of indignation, saw, as he thought, one of the passengers behind the pilot; and the passenger was Pusey.

As the plane banked and climbed, McGregor clambered from his hatch with an ancient, double-barrelled shotgun. The Skipper shouted, 'If he does it again, give him both barrels!'

But there was no cause for bloodshed. The plane, climbing steadily in the hard sunlight, flew down the loch until it was lost to sight and the engine was only a faint receding drone. As the crew of the *Maggie* stared into the distance they waited in silence, loth to voice the fear they all had. At last the boy said, 'Captain, sir. Did ye no' see who was in it?'

The Skipper shook his head. 'I've no' got eyes of a hawk, laddie.'

'But, sir, I looked. I saw him plainly. It was Mr Pusey.'

'Mr Pusey!' They laughed unconvincingly. 'And what would he be doing in an airplane?'

'Trying to stop us, maybe.'

The Skipper shuffled uneasily. He cleared his throat. 'If that was Pusey, it'd be Mr Marshall, the boss, with him.'

'Aye, that's right.'

'It was Mr Marshall, yon master at Greenock said, would be wanting us to put in for unloading.'

'Aye, that's right.'

They stood thoughtfully, side by side, while the *Maggie* chugged forward on her own erratic course. There was the possibility here of danger, all their plans could be defeated, but the Skipper was not the man to meet trouble halfway. He slapped McGregor heartily on the back. 'Och, what's there to worry about? He'd no be able to stop us even if it was Marshall, even if he wanted to.'

The boy said reasonably, 'They flew south. Would they no' be making for Campbeltown?'

'Campbeltown?'

'They could get a car there.'

'What for?'

'To catch up wi' us before we get through the Crinan Canal.'

Once again there was silence as his seniors thought their way out of an unpleasant probability. The mate flicked absent-mindedly at a seagull that was watching them from the rail. A yacht went about suddenly to escape their bows. 'Where the hell are ye steering?'

McGregor said, 'They'd never make it. By road it's forty miles.'

'Nearer fifty,' the mate said.

'By road they'll be travelling faster than us,' the boy said.

'Even if they walk it,' the Skipper said, looking at the engineman. Then, before their previous argument could develop, he added cheerfully, 'Ach, I'm thinking that couldna have been Mr Marshall. But if it was he'll have seen how far we've come already. He'll know he's got nothing to worry about. Anyway, once we're into the canal we'll be safe enough.'

The boy shook his head as he picked up his pail and scrubbing brush. 'Still, if he's troubled to hire a plane . . .'

The Skipper ruffled his hair. 'Ach, ye worry too much. The *Maggie*'s not a ship that responds well to pessimism.'

As they steamed slowly up Loch Fyne towards Ardrishaig it seemed that the Skipper's confidence would be justified. The *Maggie* was a steady as a liner on the still water. The sun was really hot despite the breeze, and there were no further signs of pursuit, real or imagined. Towards mid-afternoon they entered the Crinan Canal and now with the surface as smooth as an arterial road their passage was even more pleasant.

From a landsman's point of view, from one of the crofter's cottages that lay half hidden among the heather and the gorse, the *Maggie* presented a strange, almost fantastic, sight. With her big funnel, her derricks, her unusual outline, she moved across the scene of moorland, meadows, a copse of pine trees, the distant mountains, and it might be only the weird music of the mate's concertina, or the steady beat of the engine, that would tell an onlooker a ship was crossing the landscape.

On deck the industrious boy was now washing some clothes in a bucket. The mate was still stretched on the deck. Suddenly the afternoon quiet was broken by the clear, metallic cackling of a pheasant. The boy held up a hand, but the mate, too, had heard. They looked towards the woods, exchanged meaning glances, and then turned appealingly towards the Skipper.

The Skipper was looking over their heads, to a copse where a fine-looking pheasant strutted through the undergrowth. The Skipper jabbed thoughtfully at his pipe. He said, 'Aye, ship's stores are getting a bit low. But I wouldn't want to see ye taking other people's property.' He slowly turned his back on them. 'No. If you take other people's property, I wouldn't want to see it.'

A happy grin of anticipation brightened the boy's face. As he turned he saw that the mate was already at the derrick. They lowered the boom and, as the Skipper slowed down and steered as close to the canal bank as the depth of water would allow, they leaned over and swung out across the bank. McGregor, who had been too near his engines to hear the pheasant, saw at once what was happening and threw his shotgun down to the mate. As the *Maggie* moved slowly along the canal the mate and the boy ducked into the copse.

Turning a guileless face from the impending crime the Skipper sang happily in his wheelhouse. 'I'm ower young to marry . . .' McGregor, governing the engine to its lowest speed, anticipated the taste and smell of pheasant. Two happy men without a care in the world.

The *Maggie* was now sailing calmly towards a point where the canal narrowed at a small swing-bridge. A little, grey-haired woman was turning the handle. 'I'm ower young to marry . . .'

Just then McGregor saw the car which had stopped beside the bridge. The front doors opened – from one side the driver, from the other – Pusey!

McGregor turned in dismay towards the Skipper. 'Holy smoke!' he said. 'They've caught us.'

Chapter Nine

As he saw the car waiting at the swing-bridge and the reception committee, headed by Pusey, the Skipper ducked involuntarily into his wheelhouse. Then he came up slowly, realising that there was no escape, and decided to brazen it out. His tough old face assumed an expression of affable innocence. He glanced sideways to the deck, but there was no support from that quarter. McGregor had gone to ground in his engine-room.

The Skipper steered slowly towards his fate. As the *Maggie* bellied through the calm sunlit water he was able to take in the whole pleasant scene; no guns or barbed wire or handcuffs to show that a criminal had been cornered – not even a policeman. Behind the car and the grey-haired old lady a cottage dozed in the afternoon sun. Roses draped themselves languidly along the low garden wall, sweet williams showed their bright mosaic, pink and red valerians glowed from the bank. Against the cottage door an ancient porch wilted beneath a cascade of honeysuckle.

From this idyllic scene one of the waiting group – Pusey – walked into the hard sunlight on the swing-bridge.

He looked down silently, with lips pursed, as the *Maggie* drifted up to him and stopped. The door of the wheelhouse opened, and the Skipper, with an ingratiating smile, called out, 'My, now, and look who's here! Mr Pusey! How are ye, sir?'

Pusey glanced back to the shadows. 'You see what kind of man he is!' The car door opened and Marshall clambered deliberately into the road. Seeing him, the Skipper thought once again of flight, but with the swing-bridge closed and the canal at this point not more than thirty feet wide he was, without a doubt, cornered. With a nervous glance towards Marshall, who was waiting with the driver and Miss Peters beside the car, he came on to the deck and clambered up to Pusey on the bridge.

He asked amiably, 'And what brings ye all the way to Crinan?' Although he was talking to Pusey he hardly expected an answer and in fact his attention at the time was concentrated over Pusey's shoulder to the group by the car. He saw Marshall watching him steadily, his eyes apparently half-closed from deep emotion. He saw Marshall take a few steps forward.

With a nervous smile the Skipper said to Pusey, 'We thought you'd returned to London, sir. We never expected to see you here. We had a bit of difficulty in Glasgow, sir; ye may have read about it in the papers. Aye, but your cargo's safe and sound. Not a scratch on it anywhere.'

At last he could bear the suspense no longer. He stepped past Pusey and walked across the bridge with outstretched hand. He smiled imbecilically. 'I don't think I've met this gentleman. Is it . . . er . . . is it by any chance himself? Mr Marshall?'

Marshall stepped like a presiding judge on to the swing-bridge. He looked at the Skipper solemnly. Then, surprisingly, he took the proffered hand. 'That's right, Captain. And it's my cargo you've got aboard this . . . this . . .' He walked the length of the bridge, ignoring Pusey and McGregor, who seemed flabbergasted at his tolerance. He pointed to the *Maggie*. '. . . this incredible-looking tub.'

Following him along the bridge the Skipper nodded good-naturedly. 'The *Maggie*? Oh, the *Maggie*'s a fine old Puffer. A coat of paint and ye'd never recognise her.' He added with a confidence that even surprised himself, 'She's a sound ship and greatly respected in the trade.'

Although Marshall's expression did not relax one muscle at this preposterous statement, he had to look away quickly before his eyes showed that he could appreciate the humour of the situation. He asked, 'Are you serious? Were you really going to take this thing to sea?'

'We'll be in Kiltarra not later than . . .' the Skipper began, but Marshall shook his head.

'You may be, but not with the cargo you're carrying now.'

'I don't think I understand ye, Mr Marshall.'

The Overseas Manager of World International Airways swung round on him suddenly. 'Now look here, I'll say nothing about your misrepresentation of fact when you showed Mr Pusey the wrong boat . . .'

The Skipper took only a second to decide his line of defence, but in that second he gathered an impression of the whole court, the judge – Marshall; prosecuting counsel – Pusey, looking pettishly offended, and Miss Peters, ready in the background with notebook and facts; court usher – the driver of the hired car. And for the defence? – McGregor watching non-committally from the engine-room hatch. 'I told the auld goat not to put into Gleska!'

The Skipper repeated innocently, 'Wrong boat, Mr Marshall?' He turned brazenly towards Pusey, who was a few paces away. 'Ye mean there was some misunderstanding.'

For a few moments it seemed that the incredible might happen. Pusey was obviously on the brink of bad language.

But his employer saved him from this indignity. Marshall said, 'All right, MacTaggart. I'll give you "E" for effort. I don't even want my fifty pounds back: it probably cost you something to get *this* far. But now you're going to turn this tub around and take it back to Ardrishaig, and there you're going to unload it so that my stuff can be put aboard a sound boat. And, furthermore, I'm putting Mr Pusey aboard to see that you do.' His jaw jutted belligerently. 'Right?'

The Skipper said, aghast, 'But, Mr Marshall, I assure ye, we're more capable of doing the job for ye! It's entirely unnecessary for ye to go to the additional expense of . . .'

'I'd rather you didn't speak of the expense,' Marshall said. 'If you knew how much you've cost me already . . .' He turned to Pusey, who was nodding with sour approval in the background. 'And look here, Pusey – if for any reason, any reason whatever, he fails to have you in Ardrishaig by five o'clock, call the police. Right?'

Pusey looked vindictively at the Skipper. 'Yes, sir.'

Marshall said, 'Spend the night in Ardrishaig if necessary, but see the stuff safely loaded on the other boat. I'll expect you back in London sometime tomorrow.'

'Yes, sir.'

With the situation under control at last Marshall had another incredulous look at the *Maggie*. Then with a glance towards the Skipper he went, shaking his head, towards Miss Peters and the waiting car.

Chapter Ten

With an unbearable air of superiority Pusey watched the Skipper in his hour of defeat. Standing dismally against the bridge he was looking at the hired car jolting down the canal road as though even now by some miracle Mr Marshall might relent and allow the *Maggie* to proceed. But there was no respite. The car disappeared round a belt of trees and for a few moments a cloud of dust hung in the still air. The old lady, realising that they did not want her to open the bridge, went slowly back to her cottage. Pusey remained as victor of the field.

He said, 'Are we ready to proceed?'

The Skipper turned and came towards him reluctantly. He stood on the bridge and looked with disgust down the canal glistening in the sunlight. But he made no move towards the *Maggie*.

Pusey asked petulantly, 'I *said*: Are we ready to proceed?'

The Skipper answered gruffly, 'We canna go yet.'

'And why not?'

'We're waiting for the mate and the boy.'

'And,' Pusey asked, in a superior voice, 'where are the mate and the boy?'

The Skipper did not reply, but Pusey, who now wouldn't trust him an inch, saw him exchange glances with the engineman. It seemed that they were looking anxiously towards the woods which flanked the canal road.

'Where *are* the mate and the boy?'

As if in reply two shots sounded from the woods. Although muffled by the trees they were obviously not far away, and the Skipper, as though careless now of the consequences, nodded towards a wooded hill astern.

Pusey turned, but could see no movement in the peaceful countryside: the silent road, a copse of trees, the rising hill, and, in the distance, a line of purple mountains. He asked, 'Where are they? What are they doing?' The Skipper turned away and in a moment another shot sounded, nearer than before. Suddenly comprehending, Pusey said, 'They're poaching!'

His indignation seemed to amuse the Skipper and the engineman. The Skipper was grinning as he climbed on to the *Maggie*. 'That's an ugly word, Mr Pusey. Out here we have more delicacy. We call it "The Sport".'

'I don't see anything amusing in breaking the law,' Pusey said, in his Sunday-school voice.

They watched in silence for the mate and the boy to appear, but there was still no movement. They heard a distant shout and then a faint crackle that might have been someone walking through the dry undergrowth. A rabbit hopped out on to the road and began nibbling at the grass verge. A pheasant rose in alarm and flew across the canal with clacking wings.

It seemed to Pusey that it was beneath his dignity as master of the situation to wait any longer and he said firmly, 'Very well, as they are not coming I'll go and look for them myself.' He turned towards the engineman, 'But I insist that you come with me.'

McGregor looked at the Skipper with surprise, then, catching his shrug, stepped off the boat and followed the determined Pusey down the road. When he came to the copse he looked back, but the Skipper, who was puffing slowly at his pipe, clearly did not know what to do next.

Although he was hardly dressed for a country walk Pusey jumped without hesitation into the trees and began to plod slowly uphill. It was rough going, as he soon found, and the fact that McGregor, who was following some way behind, seemed to regard him with the tolerant amusement one affords to an eccentric or a lunatic only spurred on his determination. He stumbled in the bracken, caught his smart city trousers in the brambles, but still, angry and perspiring, managed to keep going.

The hill they were climbing was rough moorland, dotted here and there with clumps of trees. As Pusey came from one of these copses on to the open heath he turned to wait for McGregor and to regain his breath. Below, like a band of gold, was the canal with the *Maggie* still moored by the bridge. He turned towards McGregor, who was still coming leisurely up the hill.

'Where can they be? They can't have gone very far.'

'Would it no' be better, Mr Pusey, to wait for them at the boat?'

Pusey would dearly have liked to agree, but he could not risk being outsmarted again. He pointed to the woods ahead. 'I'll look over here. You take that side.'

He waited until the engineman had climbed in the direction indicated, then he too climbed with weary knees against the slope. He stumbled tiredly through the woods and, finding no sign of the mate or the boy, paused where the trees were thinning on the other side. Resting with one hand against the rough bark of a pine tree he looked out over the sunlit moorland beyond, and then, suddenly, two figures moved into his vision. At first he assumed that they must be the crew of the *Maggie*. Then, as he saw them more distinctly, he realised that they must be connected with the estate.

Although they were some way away he could see them clearly – an elderly, angry-looking man with a shotgun, and a smaller but equally fierce man with a stick. The laird and factor? The laird's angry voice came down the hillside. 'They're here somewhere. They'll not get away this time. Go and fetch the constable.'

'Aye, sir!' The factor trudged sturdily down the hill.

It occurred to Pusey immediately that however innocent he might be it would be impolitic to show himself to the laird at that moment, so he stood discreetly hidden in the darkness beneath the trees. He knew that he had no cause for fear, but he watched thankfully as the laird, with shotgun at the ready, prowled round the further clump of trees.

Then, unexpectedly, he heard someone crashing through the undergrowth of the copse he was in. At first he thought it must be the factor. The laird had heard him too and was coming wrathfully down the hill. Pusey looked nervously as the drama moved unexpectedly in his direction. The footsteps had stopped, but then a voice, McGregor's voice, called hoarsely, 'Hamish! Hamish!'

Hearing the unmistakable sound the laird came charging downhill. Outside the copse he halted, plainly undecided where to go, but he bellowed confidently, 'I know you're in there! Come out!' McGregor did not obey. Nor did Pusey. He realised that once again he was a victim of a ridiculous mischance. But if he stayed quite still . . .

The laird was coming towards Pusey when from the further copse uphill a figure came running quickly across the open gap. He was a seaman, obviously, despite the gun in his hand and the dead pheasant. The mate! Pusey watched with agonised apprehension, terrified that the mate would not reach the cover of the trees before the laird turned. Pusey recognised him now as the man who had stood impassively on Glasgow dock as the Skipper and the engineman had tricked him into this ridiculous adventure. He was impassive still, despite the exertion of leaping downhill over the heather and gorse, laden with a heavy shotgun and a pheasant. His feet made little noise on the springy turf, and it was only when he had reached the cover of the trees that the laird heard him crashing through the undergrowth.

The laird came fearsomely back, peering into the woods, and fairly bristling with anger. 'Come on out now. It'll be better for you in the long run,' but the mate had obviously joined up with the engineman, for their heavy progress through the woods, back to the canal, could be plainly heard.

Now, obviously, was the time for Pusey to follow, but the laird was standing so close to his hiding place – only a few yards away – that he could not move without risking a burst of shotgun pellets. Besides, he was innocent!

Before he could decide what to do he saw another movement up the hill. The bushes parted and the wee boy, carrying two more pheasants, came cautiously into view. Pusey held his breath, the laird turned, but the boy was down in the long grass in an instant. Infuriated by his helplessness the laird stalked away from Pusey along the edge of the wood, and immediately the boy started a spectacular dash for freedom.

The open ground he had to cover was all downhill. The mate had crossed it in a matter of seconds although it had seemed much longer to Pusey. But the boy was severely handicapped. Two pheasants were almost as much as he could carry, his legs were shorter than the mate's, and the laird, furiously angry, was now thoroughly aroused. Pusey watched in agony as the boy burst down the steep slope. He ran a few yards and then, just as the laird was turning, tripped forward into the heather. He picked himself up cautiously, but the laird had turned his back again. The boy ran on.

He came into the copse like a small thunderbolt and ran straight into Pusey's arms.

He whispered hoarsely, 'Mr Pusey! What are you . . . ?'

Pusey said, 'You're to come back to the boat at once.'

The boy looked fearfully over his shoulder. 'Ssssh! He'll hear us!'

'Did you hear what I said? The boat is returning to Ardrishaig at once!'

They both turned, sensing danger, as the laird came cautiously into the woods. He was coming directly towards them but apparently had not seen them yet.

The boy seized Pusey's arm and tried to pull him into hiding behind a fallen tree trunk.

Pusey protested, 'Take your hands off . . .'

'Ssssh!' the boy whispered urgently. 'It's the laird.' Using all his force he dragged Pusey to his knees. 'If we're caught, it's the jail for us!'

Pusey said, 'I don't care if . . .' He broke off, suddenly alarmed. Then with a show of confidence he added, 'I'll not be a party to illegal . . .'

The laird was only thirty yards away now, and by descending more steeply than they had expected he had partially cut off their retreat.

'Here he comes,' the boy said. 'Get down!'

'But this is . . .'

'Get *down*! If he catches us we'll never get away at all.'

Pusey muttered, 'This is absolutely ridiculous,' but as he saw the laird's red and angry face his false courage deserted him. He dropped beside the boy in the cover of the fallen trees.

'Come out! You can't escape! Come out!'

Pusey, with his face pressed to the earth, listened in amazement and horror.

Chapter Eleven

Seldom in Pusey's blameless life can a single half-hour have been so fraught with anguish. From the moment when he lay on the damp earth behind the tree trunk, with ants crawling over his ankles, the angry laird, armed with a shotgun, only a few yards away, he knew that once again he had allowed himself to be drawn into an indefensible position. If Mr Marshall heard . . . ! He wriggled despairingly as the ants began to crawl up his legs and was rebuked by the boy – 'Ssssh!' The laird, realising that the poachers were cornered at last, could afford to wait, and in fact it wasn't long before the factor's shout came faintly through the woods.

'Sir George! Where are ye, sir?'

The laird bellowed with the full force of his lungs, 'Over here! This way!'

From his hiding place Pusey watched with growing apprehension. Common sense told him that there could be no escape, but while there was even a faint hope . . . He was in quite incredible discomfort. Exploring ants had reached the ridge of his knee, he was bathed in perspiration, but he dared not wriggle.

'Over here!' The laird's battle-cry struck terror in his suburban mind.

Then, coming slowly up the hill, he saw the factor, still armed with his heavy stick, still looking utterly ferocious. Trailing behind was a stout constable.

'Where are ye, Sir George?'

The laird went bellowing along the wood and the boy, with the keen eye of an opportunist, saw that this might be a chance. He whispered to Pusey, 'When he gets around those bushes, run for it.'

They waited tensely, and then as the laird went momentarily out of view they scrambled to their knees. They rose cautiously to their feet. For the moment they were hidden.

Pusey heard the boy say, 'Here, I've too much to carry. Don't leave it. If they find it, we're done,' and he looked stupidly down at the pheasant he was holding. Before he could appreciate this further danger the boy was off down the hill and the laird's bellow came booming through the trees.

'Over there!'

Pusey looked wildly at the pheasant. He made as if to throw it down, then, remembering the boy's warning, decided to hold it.

'There's another one of them there. A man. Get him!'

The laird's frantic order was the last ingredient for panic. Pusey turned and ran for his life down the hill.

It was many years since he had run more than a few yards for a bus or a train, and he was gratified, almost exhilarated, by his astonishing turn of speed. Once he had started down the steep hill he had only to keep his feet and nothing could catch him. He ran, stumbled, leaped; he warded himself from trees with his free hand. His jacket was open, his tie flying to the wind. Brambles, bracken, sticks, hidden trunks, were traversed with only a minor damage to his person and rather more serious damage to his shoes and trousers.

'They're getting away! After them!' The laird's cry spurred him on. The boy was not far ahead now. He could see him running out of the woods into the patch of sunlight beside the canal.

'After them!'

It wasn't until Pusey reached the edge of the trees and the level ground along the canal that he realised how far he was from racing fit. Through the last of the trees he had been almost level with the boy, now, in the open, the boy seemed to spurt ahead.

As Pusey faltered, the challenge from the pursuers became more urgent. Looking frantically over his shoulder he saw the laird, still with his shotgun, gaining steadily, and behind him the factor, with the constable far in the rear. He spurted desperately for a few paces, and then with heart thumping madly had to fall into a gasping, shambling trot.

He wasted another precious second by looking back. The laird was close behind now. He could see his ferocious expression and the beaded sweat on his brow. Far behind, the factor had dropped out of the hunt and was being comforted by the constable.

Pusey knew that he couldn't last much longer. Above his own laboured breath and the thumping of his heart he could hear the determined grunting of the laird. He staggered wildly and only just saved himself from falling. Then, at last, he realised that he was still clutching the pheasant. He flung it violently away, and protested with his last gasping breath, 'This has nothing to do with me!'

The next moment he felt the laird's clutching hand at his shoulder, and they were wrestling on the bank of the canal.

'Hold on, Sir George! I'm coming!'

Stung to a last effort by the factor's cry Pusey struggled away. The laird, who was also near exhaustion, held him grimly by the lapel.

Then with a resounding tear the lapel ripped away from the coat. Thrown off balance the laird staggered, balanced for an interminable moment with flailing arms, before falling backwards over the canal bank.

He hit the water with a terrible splash. He submerged and came up gasping, 'Help! I can't swim! Help!'

Pusey, who had run a few paces along the bank, hesitated. Then, seeing that the factor and the constable were still some distance away, he knelt on the bank and extended a hand.

His worst failing, as Mr Marshall had often told him, was not knowing his own mind. Just as the laird made a frantic grab, Pusey realised that the factor and constable must catch him before he could drag the laird from the water. He withdrew his hand hurriedly and the laird went under for the second time.

By this time the factor had reached the point on the canal bank and Pusey had staggered a few paces towards freedom. The factor knelt, as Pusey had done, and extended his hand. But the laird's instinct for self-preservation was confused with an even stronger emotion, a desire to murder Pusey. Still floundering and thrashing the water, he yelled hysterically, 'Arrest that man! Arrest . . .' The rest was lost as he sank for the third time.

The unfortunate Pusey had everything against him to the last. Hearing the shout he made the mistake of glancing back. At that moment his weary feet caught on a stone and he fell heavily in the dust.

As he looked up, with all fight gone, he saw the laird being dragged from the water. Although the laird was quite unable to speak he could still gesticulate. He made violent signs at Pusey, and the factor, understanding, left the constable to complete the rescue.

Pusey, who had twisted his ankle, was soon overtaken by the furious factor. Too weak, too lame, too breathless to resist, he waited humbly for the last indignities of fate.

Chapter Twelve

(1)

In his suite at the Central in Glasgow, Marshall was preparing to leave. The small adventure was over, and, by catching the night train, he would only have lost one day. It was quite a story in its way – worth telling to Johnson and Vanders, and young Blair of Asiatic Chemicals. He jotted a note of the Skipper's name while he remembered it – MacTaggart. Foolish to spoil a story by forgetting the details. MacTaggart: now there was a man!

The door of his room was open and he heard Miss Peters opening the outer door.

'Oh, good evening.'

A voice he remembered, the voice of the reporter Fraser. 'Good evening. My editor said Mr Marshall wanted me to stop by and . . .'

He called out, 'Come in, Mr Fraser.'

The young man came in diffidently, and yet with a certain eagerness as though, even now, there might be some unexpected twist to what he called in his newspaper

'The Puffer Story'. You never knew with a man like MacTaggart. You could never say the story was finished until the old man was dead or safely under lock and key. Even then . . .

Marshall was saying, 'Well, Mr Fraser . . .' He broke off as he saw his secretary. She asked, 'If you don't want anything else, Mr Marshall . . .'

Marshall nodded. 'That's all right, Miss Peters. If you could call me half an hour before train time.' From the relaxed tone of his voice the reporter knew that everything had been settled. MacTaggart had been beaten. The Puffer Story was finished. He felt something more than disappointment – resentment, animosity almost, towards this sleek, efficient American, with his secretary, his public relations officer, his expensive clothes, bottles of Vichy water . . . the power of money.

Marshall was holding up the evening copy of the *Star*. 'Well, now, Mr Fraser, I ask you. Don't you think this is a little too much?'

'Too much, Mr Marshall?'

The American leaned across the table. 'Look, yesterday you had a good laugh at my expense, and I let it ride. But there's no need to make me out a complete fool, is there?'

'I certainly didn't intend to be offensive, sir.'

'I'm not saying you did. But you seem to be trying to make a *career* out of my difficulties. Why?'

The reporter explained seriously. 'You don't understand, Mr Marshall. These old Puffers are public characters in Scotland. They're news when anything happens to them. They're not much to look at but they're popular . . .'

'Well, they're not very popular with me!'

'No, sir, but they are held in great . . . I won't say esteem, but . . . well, people like them. We build big liners up here, Mr Marshall, the biggest in the world. But the Puffer's the little chap. The public always likes the little chap.'

In the other room a telephone started to ring. It went on ringing as Marshall continued to speak.

He said, 'That man MacTaggart is an out-and-out scoundrel, and you know it! That tub of his is a disgrace. But you seem to get a big kick out of it. You seem mighty glad when he gets away with murder!'

The reporter gave a disarming grin. 'Oh, yes, indeed, sir.'

'Well, Fraser, I can take a joke as well as the next man, but there's nothing very funny about this . . .' He broke off in annoyance, realising that Miss Peters had gone and that the telephone was still ringing in the other room. He walked masterfully to the door. The outer room was empty, but the telephone kept on with its shrill 'Brr-brr: brr-brr' as though it hardly cared that it was disturbing Mr Calvin B. Marshall.

'Just one moment.' Marshall strode up to the telephone.

'Hallo, hallo. Yes. Marshall speaking.' His frigid voice thawed a little. 'Oh, Mr Campbell, what can I do for you?'

The broad Scottish voice touched with a note of humour came over the wires: 'I'm sorry to disturb you, Mr Marshall, but I've just had a message from Captain Anderson at Ardrishaig. He says he hasn't been contacted by anybody. The *Maggie* hasn't returned.'

Marshall's confidence, built up by years of efficiency and success, was roughly shaken. He tried to think, but another telephone was ringing now, the one in the room he had just left. He hesitated, undecided, and then seeing the reporter's enquiring gesture, he nodded for him to answer it.

He turned back to the telephone he was holding. 'But – I don't understand. It's almost ten o'clock. There must be some mistake.'

'There's no mistake, Mr Marshall.'

'But Pusey is actually on board the thing. How could they . . . ?' He stopped and looked towards Fraser, who had come to the adjoining door.

Fraser said, 'Mr Pusey is on the other line.'

'Well, thank goodness!' He spoke into his telephone, 'Hang on a second, Mr Campbell. Pusey's just rung in . . .' He laid down the receiver and hurried into the inner room.

As he picked up the other phone he saw the reporter watching him intently, expectantly. He thought to himself, 'Whatever's happened I must keep calm. I must keep calm!'

'Hello, Pusey. It's about time. Have you started loading the stuff? *What*? Well, where are you? But, Pusey, all I wanted you to do was to see that . . . *Pusey, how could you possibly have been arrested for poaching!*'

He was too astonished, too worried, to feel angry that the reporter was watching him with an expression of incredulous delight.

(2)

In the cottage jail beside the Crinan Canal Pusey, looking haggard and drawn, was bleating into the telephone. Beside him the constable listened patiently to the conversation.

'Yes, sir . . . Yes, Mr Marshall . . . Thank you, sir . . . I will, Mr Marshall . . . Yes, Mr Marshall . . . Good . . .'

As Marshall rang off, Pusey replaced the receiver. He looked quite demented with worry. His lips moved nervously.

Then, pulling himself together, he turned on the constable. 'That was Mr Marshall, the Overseas Manager of World International Airways. He's going to contact our legal department immediately. We'll soon see whether I'm to remain in this . . .'

The constable held out a large, matter-of-fact hand. 'That'll be three shillings, sir.'

'Oh!' Pusey paid the money with a bad grace. Then he saw where the constable was leading – a small room furnished with nothing but a bed and with its single window barred. 'Why can't I take a room at the inn?'

The constable said kindly, 'I'm afraid ye'll have to stay where ye are until tomorrow morning when the Magistrate's ready to see ye.'

Pusey protested angrily. 'I won't stand for this! I demand to speak to the Magistrate himself, and at once! Who is the Magistrate, anyway?'

The constable said, with relish, 'He's the laird that you pushed into the canal.'

Chapter Thirteen

(1)

The airplane tore across the runway and whipped angrily at the dust as it climbed into the air. The hedgerows, the tall trees, even the massive electric pylons, seemed to cringe beneath its fury. Up steeply; the road, the river, gardens, fields, the whole town of Renfrew, lay prostrate below. Against the urgent wind it struck with irresistible might. Then, still full of roaring anger, it turned towards the sea.

Beside the pilot Marshall sat in grim silence. A map was spread out on his knees, and every few minutes he traced some landmark – a hill, a village, the beginning of a loch – as though he was not in a mood to trust anyone. When he was certain that they were on the right course he picked up a newspaper, the *Star*, and a note on CSS letter-paper fell out.

'I'm afraid that the cargo must be aboard our boat by tomorrow afternoon, otherwise it will be necessary for you to make other arrangements.

Yours sincerely,

J. CAMPBELL.'

As he screwed up the letter the newspaper headlines caught his attention. 'THE PUFFER ESCAPES AGAIN.' He withdrew into pleasant consideration of what he would do to MacTaggart.

The pilot, a cheerfully obtuse young man, asked, 'What kind of a boat is it you're trying to catch?' He did not see Marshall's expression and he went on, 'Is it a Puffer by any chance?'

Marshall grunted, but the pilot took this to mean, 'Yes.'

He said, with interest, 'Is it now? Ach, they're wonderful boats, the old Puffers. Did you read in the paper about the one that got caught on the subway?'

Marshall, who had lost all sense of humour, looked bleakly ahead.

The pilot said, 'MacTaggart, the skipper is. Ah, there's a man for ye! What a reputation he's got! Only last month, in Campbeltown, I seen him so drunk . . . ye wouldna believe!'

Marshall sat up alertly as he saw the long blue sausage of the loch. 'This is it.'

They dived sharply, like a kestrel on the kill, and the tiny boats lay defenceless on the expanse of water. As they pulled out of the dive they passed a ferry boat with a few passengers at the stern waving gaily. Then, keeping a level course above the blue rippled water they saw a big cargo boat, a tanker.

'There she is!'

They came down low and flew alongside the *Maggie*.

'It's her all right.'

As the pilot pulled the plane into a steady climb Marshall studied his map.

'Let's see . . .' He asked the pilot, 'Where do you reckon they're making for?'

The pilot put his finger on the map. 'It looks like they're putting into Inverkerran for the night.'

Marshall looked back speculatively at the *Maggie*, which was now only a dot on the expanse of blue. He said, 'Tell me: if they thought *I* was going to Inverkerran, where do you reckon they would make for then?'

The pilot considered. 'Strathcathaigh, maybe.'

Marshall frowned. 'Look – this sounds silly, but if they thought I'd think they were going to Strathcathaigh because it looked as if they were going to Inverkerran – where would they make for then?'

'My guess would be Pennymaddy.'

Marshall nodded wearily. 'Well, if there's such a thing as a triple bluff, I'll bet MacTaggart invented it. Okay, Pennymaddy it is.'

(2)

When they saw the plane the crew of the *Maggie* knew without doubt that they had been discovered. They watched it dive, a mile or two along the loch, then as it came low over the water, passing close to each boat in turn, they knew that it would not be long before it came to them. They turned in a slow, swinging arc as it flew alongside. Finally, as it rose again and flew off, they looked at each other with apprehension.

The Skipper was scratching his beard. 'Aye, he'll have guessed we were making for Inverkerran.'

The mate asked, 'Will he no' go there himself, then?'

The Skipper shook his head. 'Och, no. He'll know *we* know he's seen us. So he'll be expecting us to make for Strathcathaigh instead.'

The mate said, 'Well, shall I set her for Pennymaddy, then?'

'No. Because if it should occur to *him* that it's occurred to *us* that he'd be expecting us to make for Strathcathaigh he'd be thinking we'd make for Pennymaddy.'

'Well, shall I set her for Pinwhinnoich?'

The Skipper smiled and relaxed. 'Och, no. We'll make for Inverkerran, just the way we planned. It's the last place he'd be likely to think of.'

(3)

The airplane came down at Ardramessan, which was the nearest landing field to Pennymaddy. Marshall paid off the pilot, who facetiously wished him, 'Good luck, sir. You'll need it all!' He hired a car to take him to Pennymaddy. After his experience with the pilot he sat anxiously beside the driver, jolting over the bad roads, suffering at each bump from a broken spring, waiting to see whether his companion was also a talker. He was. Knowing every curve and twist and hole in the road he could afford to give all his garrulous attention to his passenger. When they reached Pennymaddy Marshall could feel the threat of a nervous breakdown.

He climbed stiffly out and walked along the jetty. 'Wait here. I'll have to see . . . I may need you again.'

They waited two hours before it was clear that the *Maggie* was not coming there for the night.

Marshall climbed grimly back into the car.

'Where will it be now, sir?'

'Strarcashay.'

'Where, sir?'

'Strarcashay.'

The driver laughed aloud, despite his passenger's hunched shoulders and heavy frown. 'Oh no, sir. You mean Strathcathaigh.'

'Whatever I mean, let's go there.'

Once more they jolted over roads that might have caused the most good-natured man to ride in silence. But not the driver. He came from a large family and his wife came from a large family. It seemed to Marshall that no one could reasonably have so many relations or know so much about their intimate lives. It was a relief to reach Strathcathaigh.

His pleasure at leaving the driver, even for a few minutes, was diluted by the fact that the *Maggie* was not in the harbour. Marshall swore softly. He thought of the bad roads, the broken spring, the driver's relations. Any lesser man would have given up.

Marshall clenched his jaw and marched back to the car.

'It's a pretty place, sir – Strathcathaigh. Where would ye like to be going now?'

'Inverkerran – in silence!'

The long shadows were falling across the road as they came at last to the small fishing village of Inverkerran. Outside the cottages men in blue jerseys sat smoking in the evening sun. A fisherman was folding his nets. A dog barked at the seagulls on the shore.

The car stopped. 'This is Inverkerran, sir.'

Marshall climbed wearily out and hobbled across the narrow street. He looked down at the boats in the harbour and instantly his expression changed to one of almost diabolical satisfaction. Riding gently on the deep water by the harbour wall was the *Maggie*.

Chapter Fourteen

Marshall walked quickly back to the hired car. He looked suspiciously up the single street of the village as though even now the *Maggie*'s crew might see him and escape. In an open doorway a small ragged-trousered boy stood with one hand against the lintel, the old fishermen watched as they puffed slowly at their pipes, a cat slunk nervously along a wall.

The car driver was leaning cheerfully out of his window. Marshall asked, 'Okay. What do I owe you?'

The driver recaptured on his fingers the points of their nightmare journey. 'Ardramessan to Pennymaddy, Pennymaddy to Strathcathaigh, Strathcathaigh to Inverkerran . . . That'll be twelve pounds, sir.'

'Twelve pounds!' Marshall took out his pocket book and grimly counted the notes. 'Well, there's five pounds – and seven pounds for yourself. Right?'

The driver smiled in an infuriating way and drove off up the village street. As it bumped and rattled across the cobbles Marshall could see, from the tilt of the chassis, just how badly the spring was broken.

He turned briskly towards the harbour. A stone jetty stretched like a curving finger into the grey water, and, alongside, the *Maggie* rode gently on the swell. She looked deserted, but Marshall was determined to take no chances. Although there was no one on deck or in the wheelhouse, and the hawsers were still round the bollards, he did not let his attention wander for one second as he stepped cautiously along the pier. Once he was on board . . .

He came to the ladder and stepped quietly down on to the deck. The boat really did look deserted. He walked to the aft hatchway and called, 'MacTaggart!'

He walked to the other hatch. '*You* – down there!'

There was no movement or acknowledgment. It occurred to him that if he went down into the cabin, where they might well be hiding, they would have a chance to escape. Only a few seconds, but enough, he knew, for MacTaggart's men. He decided to wait on deck.

The minutes passed and the half-hour. Light was fading across the water and an evening mist was shrouding the mountains. A lamp appeared in a cottage window, and a mother's voice called angrily, 'Wully – come to bed!' Waiting with grim determination on the wooden steps, Marshall wondered whether he was being overcautious. If the crew really were hiding on board they were showing more patience than he would have considered possible. MacTaggart, for instance, might be a canny man, a wolf hiding his cunning beneath the innocent visage of a sheep, but patient . . .? He went to the hatch of the captain's cabin and shouted, 'Hi there! MacTaggart!' But there was no movement or sound other than the gentle slap-slap of water against the stone jetty and the creak of rope against wood.

Marshall climbed awkwardly down the steps into the cabin. Quite deserted. Two bunks – both unmade, a table littered with rubbish, a rickety chair, a whisky bottle – almost empty, dirty glasses, a pack of cards. The air was stale with tobacco smoke. The other cabin was also deserted, also unkempt. In the engine-room Marshall paused for a moment, looking round with an engineer's interest. He came up shaking his head. To think that his cargo might have been risked on this! Of one thing he was certain: the *Maggie* would founder in the first storm. It was a miracle of luck, or, he admitted grudgingly, of seamanship, that she had remained afloat for so long.

Now that he was sure that MacTaggart could not escape he began to think of other things – of food and drink, of soap and water and a clean towel. From the deck he could see the cottages straggling along the water's edge and one larger building with a metal sign on the wall – the inn. He climbed up on to the jetty.

As he walked briskly towards food and warmth he noted in his suspicious mind a boy who had come down on to the jetty. The boy seemed to be coming along towards the *Maggie*, but as he saw Marshall he hesitated. It took a few seconds for this fact to register properly with Marshall. Then he stopped suspiciously and looked back. He remembered a boy's magazine in one of the cabins.

As he stopped, the boy instantly changed course, away from the *Maggie*. With an elaborate air of innocence he began to walk away from it, kicking a stone and circling to get back towards the village. He passed Marshall, stopped with an obviously pretended interest by an upturned rowing-boat, and then sauntered casually back the way he had come.

Marshall moved after him. He called, 'Hey, sonny!'

The boy walked on, pretending not to hear.

'Hey!'

The boy glanced back, and hesitated, but as Marshall came towards him he started to walk away more quickly. Marshall quickened his step and the boy broke into a trot. Marshall followed at a run.

They came at a hard canter to the village pub. The boy turned the corner quickly with Marshall some twenty yards in the rear. As the boy ducked into the back door Marshall was coming down the side path. He went past the back door, round the next corner until he came again to the village street. He looked round cautiously and was just in time to see the Skipper and the engineman and the wee boy come dashing out of the front door and start on another circular tour. Marshall followed with grim pleasure.

They were obviously not aware that he had seen them, and as he came round for the second time to the back of the pub he saw them trying in vain to wriggle out of sight behind a rhubarb patch. He stared at them in amazement. Even an ostrich had as much sense as this! The meagre cover would not have hidden a baby.

As he came slowly forward the Skipper, realising at last that he was cornered, raised his head and looked wildly around. There was no escape. Then, rising and coming forward with outstretched hand, he said, in a tone of astonishment such as he might have used to greet a friend met casually in a Glasgow street, 'Well, look who's here! If it isna Mr Marshall himself!'

With the half-ashamed air of schoolboys caught in an apple orchard they followed Marshall back to a telephone booth near the harbour. Hamish, the mate, scenting trouble, came from a cottage to join them. Darkness was settling in earnest now, and Marshall had difficulty in making his arrangements in the cramped area of the box. He was a big man and he found that there was scarcely room for a briefcase and map as well as himself. When he had found the number of the CSS offices in Glasgow he dropped the map; then he dropped the briefcase; the telephone flex was hopelessly entangled; the papers in his briefcase spilled on to the floor and he had to open the door with his buttocks before he could bend sufficiently to pick them up. The operator pretended not to understand his American burr.

'Hello, hello! Is that the CSS office?'

At last he was connected with Campbell, and, with the frantic urgency of one who cannot rest until the least possibility of disaster is averted, he made his arrangements. Round the box, in the thickening gloom, the Skipper and the engineman, the mate and the wee boy hovered like vampires.

Marshall was shouting, 'Yes, I've caught them — at Inverkerran. How soon can the other boat get here? Oban? — Yes, Mr Campbell, but that . . . I'd have to sail on the thing myself. I'm not letting those lunatics out of my sight — oh, all right, if it will save a whole day . . . Don't worry. It'll be there – what? What's that? Yes, just a moment, operator.' He opened the door quickly. 'Give me a shilling, will you?'

The Skipper fished deeply into his pocket and pulled out a few coppers and a wad of tobacco. He turned to McGregor and the mate but they hadn't a shilling between them. They all looked at the boy, who reluctantly began to empty his pockets – a clasp-knife, a magazine, a half-eaten apple. Marshall hesitated, then shouted into the receiver, 'It'll be there.'

He slammed down the receiver, and started down the jetty towards the *Maggie*. He seemed too angry to speak, and the crew followed him in glum silence. But the Skipper could not be downcast for long. He lengthened his stride and came up to Marshall's shoulder.

He asked, 'But is it worth your while to go thirty miles south, Mr Marshall?'

Marshall did not even turn his head, but the Skipper went on undaunted.

'It's sailing in the wrong direction, d'ye realise? And we could reach Kiltarra in two days easy, just like . . .'

Still Marshall did not look round, but he interrupted in a voice carefully controlled, as though he were speaking to a child. Obviously he was still very angry.

Marshall said, 'MacTaggart, I can think of nineteen reasons why I should have you put in jail. You took fifty pounds under false pretences. You got Pusey arrested for poaching. You cost me two days' worth of airplanes at sixteen pounds an hour and enough on taxis to buy a fleet of taxis . . .'

The Skipper was genuinely sorry. He said, 'If I've offended ye in any way . . .'

Marshall raised his hands to heaven and started to climb down the steps to the *Maggie*. After he had climbed four or five rungs he looked up at the Skipper's guileless countenance. With a terrible effort of self-restraint he said, 'But if you want to know the real reason I'm taking this cargo away from you, it's simply that nobody ever gets away with trying to make a monkey out of me!'

Chapter Fifteen

In the captain's cabin Marshall was trying to recapture some of the time lost on this crazy adventure. Seated on a rickety chair he had spread the papers in his briefcase over the small table. The oil lamp above his head gave a meagre light. All evening he had been sitting here, on guard, trying to concentrate on his work, while the boat rose to the swelling tide, rose and fell, rose and fell. He tried not to think of tomorrow, when they must put to sea. He stood up irritably and tried to turn up the lamp wick. Normally he could concentrate anywhere – in a car, a train, a moving plane. But here in the silent harbour, with only the slapping waves, the bark of a dog, an occasional burst of song from the inn, he found himself turning the same problems over and over in his mind. He leaned back tiredly in the chair. You couldn't carry efficiency in a briefcase. Then he sat up, determined not to be beaten. There were two whole days to be made up. Two whole days!

For a few minutes he drove his tired brain forward. Then, at a distant but unmistakable sound, he hesitated again. Someone was coming along the jetty, someone singing. With laboured patience Marshall put down his pen.

There were several minutes of scuffling and puffing before the Skipper got safely on to the *Maggie*. He was singing again as he negotiated the deck.

'I'm ower young to marry yet . . .'

Listening tensely Marshall heard him stumble over a bucket, fall, rise unsteadily, and stagger towards the lighted cowling of the hatch.

> 'I'm ower young to marry yet,
> I'm ower young to marry.'

He came slowly and with great difficulty down the ladder into the cabin, first his feet, then his legs, his whole swaying body. He reached safety at last and turned with expansive generosity and good nature towards his guest.

'D'ye know any of the old airs, Mr Marshall?' He sang in a melancholy voice, 'I'm ower young to marry yet – hic.' He steadied himself against the table. 'Ach, ye should have come with us. We'd soon learn ye . . .'

Unable to escape from the tiny cabin Marshall had his hand gripped warmly in the Skipper's rough palm. MacTaggart said, with emotion, 'I have been thinking about our small dispute of this evening, sir, and I realise that you spoke in anger. A bit of luck with the weather, and we'll be sailing along to Glenbrachan just as smart as ye please.'

He seemed to sense that Marshall did not want to be embraced. He looked vaguely round the cabin, trying to concentrate, in the aura of whisky, on what he was saying. He took two steps towards his bunk, sat down and made a half-hearted attempt to unfasten a bootlace.

He continued, in a deep voice, slurring his words, 'She's a bonny wee boat, a bonny wee boat right enough. Aye, I was born aboard her, Mr Marshall, sixty-one years ago. Did ye know that? Born aboard the old *Maggie*. Aye, and I'll die aboard her, too . . .'

He leant back happily, his speech becoming more and more indistinct as he added, 'After a respectable . . . interval.' He passed into oblivion.

Marshall picked up his pen and tried to concentrate on his work again. He frowned as he sorted out his papers. He fumbled in his briefcase.

Like a bluebottle round the bone of his concentration the Skipper's voice mumbled incoherently, drifted after a while into heavy breathing, and then became a series of vibrating snores.

Infuriated beyond words, Marshall turned towards the recumbent figure on the bunk. The snores came from the very depths of slumber, rose, inflated, rattled out their challenge and died again into a brittle silence. For a few seconds there was a lull before the next one began. The smell of whisky seemed almost tangible in the small cabin. Marshall struggled vainly to open a porthole which hadn't been opened for years. Nursing his injured hand he turned again to the unconscious Skipper, whose snores were coming smoothly now like the sound of an efficient but eccentric engine.

In exasperation Marshall shoved his papers into his briefcase, grabbed some blankets and the palliasse, and stamped up the ladder to the deck.

In the cool night air there was peace. From the cottages round the harbour a dozen lights shone warmly; the jetty was like a white path through the darkness; across the still water two cargo ships passed with winking lights. Marshall threw down the palliasse by the wheelhouse and, with a feeling of relief, sat down with the blankets wrapped round him like a cloak. In the stillness he began slowly to relax. There was nothing here to worry him, nothing he could do. Beyond any reasonable doubt he knew that the *Maggie* could not move until daybreak. He could relax and sleep.

From the forward hatchway a small gnomish head appeared. Bright eyes were watching in the darkness. The wee boy climbed on to the deck and came deferentially towards the passenger.

'Would you like a mithfa tay, sir?'

Marshall looked at him, startled. 'What?'

'Can I bring ye a mithfa tay, sir?'

Marshall turned the words over in his mind – 'A mithfa tay'. Presumably they were English, his own language. They only needed decoding.

'Can I bring ye a mithfa tay, sir?'

Marshall waved his hand testily. 'Well, whatever it is, no.' He watched the wee boy turn disappointedly towards the hatch.

Peace returned again, but not comfort. After a few minutes the deck assumed an uncanny torturing hardness, the metal rivets on the wheelhouse were small but irritating as a stone in the shoe. For thirty years Marshall had not suffered any discomfort more severe than a bumpy air crossing. Now, with flesh and bones still aching from the long car ride, he tried to wriggle first one way, then another, to find a position of comfort and sleep. This day was a complete loss. He was resigned to that. But it was essential to sleep well tonight so that at least some of tomorrow's hours might be saved. A cool breeze had sprung up and the wind blowing in from the open loch was chilling his body wherever the blankets slid away. He clutched at comfort with both hands, nestling into his blankets like a Red Indian beside a camp fire.

At last as warmth returned Marshall began to feel the first drowsy symptoms of sleep. His eyes were heavy, his thoughts blurred. It had been a long day.

Another figure came noisily from the forward hatch. This time it was the engineman with a bucket and rope. He stepped over Marshall's body and from the stern rail threw the bucket into the harbour with a resounding plop. When he drew it up, brimming with water, he clattered carelessly back across the deck, stepping over Marshall and spilling a good deal of water in the process.

Marshall stood up furiously. He looked wildly round the boat. For one moment he was tempted to find a room at the inn. Then he walked round to the other side of the wheelhouse. He opened the door. There was just room enough, he considered, for a man lying hunched up to prostrate himself on the floor. Dragging the palliasse and blankets along the deck he wondered desperately whether there would be any end to his annoyances. Sleep: all he wanted was some small corner where he could be quiet and free from interruption. Grovelling in the darkness he managed to fix up an unsatisfactory bed, but when he lay down he found that he was so tired that sleep would surely come.

At first he did not hear the mate coming along the jetty. A low murmur of conversation, a hum of lover's talk like bees on a summer afternoon; then quite definitely they were there, only a few feet from the wheelhouse – Hamish and a girl. He could hear every word they said.

'Did ye really mean what ye said, Hamish? Tell me the truth. . . . Am I really the one for you?'

Marshall opened his eyes, deliberately listening.

'Ach, ye said that the last time, and then ye went away and didn't come back for over a year . . .' There was the sound of a kiss – 'Ah, Hamish, me love . . .'

Marshall rose slowly on to his elbows.

'Do ye love me, Hamish? Oh, Hamish . . . *Hamish*.'

Marshall's face appeared slowly above the level of the window. He stared out at the couple on the wharf with the eyes of a madman.

Chapter Sixteen

In the brightness of morning Marshall felt confidence returning. Although it was only an hour since dawn the sun was already warm on the deck. The cottages, the pub, the small grey chapel, were sharply delineated in the clear air. Across the water a heat mist was rising and the distant mountains were shrouded in haze. From the harbour wall the fishermen passed slowly across the smooth loch, rowing because there was not a breath of wind to fill their sails.

'A fine morning, sir.' The Skipper, who had come to Marshall's side, seemed quite unaffected by the previous night's drinking.

Marshall looked at him with reluctant respect, the big nose, humorous eyes, the ragged beard that stuck out jauntily through every depression. 'How far is it to go?'

'To Oban, sir. Well, it's a gude long journey, a gude long journey.'

'According to my map it's only thirty miles.'

'Maybe so, maybe so.' The Skipper nodded seriously. 'But I wouldn't want to drive the auld *Maggie*, ye understand? We'll take it slow but steady.'

Marshall turned deliberately to face him. 'Look, MacTaggart. I know exactly what this old tub will do, I know she's about the slowest thing that ever put to sea, but I want my cargo in Oban *today*. Unless you go fifty miles or so off course even you can't prevent that.' He took out a small folding compass. 'But I'm warning you, I can check a straight course as well as you. So don't try any tricks!'

The Skipper turned away, offended. 'Ye don't have to speak to me like that, Mr Marshall. To go a long way off course with the deliberate intention of missing the CSS boat at Oban – why it'd be – it'd be dishonest.'

Marshall walked away to the stern. 'Well, don't run the risk that I might think that of you.'

'Of course,' the Skipper said to himself, 'there might have to be a wee deviation now and then. For rocks or a big ocean liner or maybe a shipwreck.'

The *Maggie*, with steam up, was about to go. The mate and the boy were casting off. A girl watched them wistfully from the jetty.

'Goodbye, Hamish.'

The Skipper and McGregor, who was standing beside the wheelhouse, were watching Marshall in the bows. McGregor was not like the Skipper; he could acknowledge defeat.

'Ach, what's the use?' he was saying. 'He'll have us in Oban by teatime even if we drift half the way. Fraser's boat won't be waiting to pick up his stuff before evening.'

Leaning out of his wheelhouse the Skipper said, reflectively, 'It's thirty miles to Oban. A great many things can happen in thirty miles.

McGregor took up his meaning at once. 'The engine . . . ?'

He may have spoken too loudly, for Marshall glanced back and then came along the boat to join them. 'I was just thinking,' Marshall said, 'about the things that might happen to prevent our reaching Oban by this afternoon. Engine trouble, for example.' He caught their quick, nervous glances. 'I think I should tell you, gentlemen, *I built* a better engine than that when I was eight years old.'

The Puffer moved out of harbour into the open sea. There was nothing to hinder her progress, no squall, no current, no crossing boats. They waffled steadily along some three miles off the south coast of Mull. To Marshall, sitting in the bows, it seemed that their progress was infinitesimal. The mate was reclining against the hatchway with his concertina. The boy was peeling potatoes in the galley. McGregor stood on the engine-room steps with his elbows on the deck. Only the Skipper seemed to have any part in sailing the boat, and his efforts, a slight turn of the wheel every few minutes, could hardly be called strenuous. After an hour Marshall was fuming with impatience, but there was nothing he could complain about. The bows seemed to be cutting sharply enough through the water, and the course, from frequent checkings on his compass, was correct. The boy came on to deck and listened to the mate's concertina.

'Mr Marshall, sir . . .'

Marshall turned and saw the Skipper beckoning him from the open window of his wheelhouse. He went back suspiciously. 'Well?'

The Skipper said, 'I have a feeling there's some fog coming on.'

'Fog!' Marshall looked at him in astonishment.

'It might be wise to put her in somewhere.'

'Are you serious? How on earth could you know that there was . . .'

The Skipper said vaguely, 'Well, there's the time of year, and a bit of a nip in the air after the heat, and the way the wind's fallen away . . . You might call it a seaman's instinct.'

Marshall looked round briefly at the perfectly clear sky. Then he strode angrily back to his seat in the bows. 'Fog!'

Within the hour the sea was layered with fog as thick as cotton wool. From the aft hatch the bows were invisible, and from the forward hatch they couldn't see the wheel-house. Marshall, who knew enough about the sea to recognise their danger, groped nervously about the deck. He could barely see across the width of the boat. Up in the bows he saw the distorted figures of the mate and the boy. He watched them distractedly. While the mate took soundings with a line, the boy was picking lumps of coal from a bucket beside him and throwing them with all his might into the grey nothingness ahead. After each throw he listened for the plop as the coal hit the water.

Marshall asked nervously, 'What are you doing that for?'

Hamish, the mate, turned with a grin. 'Radar!'

'What do you mean?'

The boy explained. 'So long as it plops, we're all right. But if it rattles . . .'

Marshall said, 'If it rattles, what?'

'Then we'll know we made a mistake.'

Trying to mask his fear by action Marshall groped slowly back to the wheelhouse. He was hardly reassured by the fact that the Skipper was quite unperturbed. He had already decided that MacTaggart was a madman.

'I'm taking her into Fiona Bay,' the Skipper explained calmly. 'To beach her. It's all right, sir. It's what she was built for.'

'But what makes you think you're going into Fiona Bay and not on to some rocks?'

The Skipper paused to listen to the plopping of the coal. Then he said, 'Ach, weel, I'm not sure I could explain it to ye. Ye just know.'

When the fog lifted, as suddenly as it had fallen, the *Maggie* was indeed safely beached, but in a position that made her appearance even more ludicrous than usual. She was high and dry on a sandbank, half a mile from the sea and half a mile from the shore. It would be hours before she could float from her indignity with the incoming tide.

Marshall, who had fallen asleep in the captain's cabin, was suddenly conscious that the engines were not going. He sat up with a startled expression, thinking that perhaps the boat had been abandoned, or was sinking. He looked at his watch, leaped up and tried to peer through the port-hole. But it was too dirty for him to see anything at all, except that the mist had cleared. Scrambling clumsily from the bunk he clambered up on to the deck.

He looked wildly round and saw the Skipper with McGregor and the boy talking quietly in the bows. The mate was asleep on the hatch. On all sides the sand stretched desolately away.

Marshall came up to them furiously. 'It's almost four o'clock. Why didn't you wake me?' Then, before the Skipper could speak, 'All right, it doesn't matter.' He spread out his map. 'Show me where we are on here.' As the Skipper indicated, 'Right. Where's the nearest place with a telephone?'

The Skipper said, 'Weel, ye could walk back to Inverkerran, but that's over the hill there. It would be quicker to go to Loch Mora – here.'

Marshall said, appalled, 'But that's almost ten miles!'

The Skipper shrugged sympathetically. Marshall furiously folded his map, shoved it in his pocket again and strode across the deck to the side of the ship. 'All right. Let's get going.'

The Skipper looked at him doubtfully. 'Were ye wanting me to come with you, sir?'

'You don't think I'm going to leave you here so that you can accidentally drift away again, do you?'

'Drift away, sir? The tide won't be in for hours. She's no' on wheels.'

As he glanced at the vast expanse of rippled sands, wet with sea puddles and rivulets, Marshall knew that the Skipper was right, but for once in his life he was ready to acknowledge someone smarter than himself. If there was a chance in a thousand of a double-cross the Skipper would know it. He said, 'I'd rather you came with me. A little exercise will do you good.'

The Skipper shrugged and smiled as he followed him down the rope ladder.

Across the interminable half-mile of sand Marshall plodded ahead, feeling all the time that in the eyes of MacTaggart and his crew *he* was the eccentric. To them his need for speed and efficiency was quite incredible. Given good weather and their own peculiar knowledge of these western lochs and isles they would have proceeded happily enough, at three or four knots, until with God's good grace they might even have reached Kiltarra. A few days, a few weeks: what did it matter?

Well, to Marshall it mattered a great deal. All his life he had requested and understood the power of money. Now, with his marriage breaking up, he was going to try to buy back his young wife's love. At Kiltarra, in the Western Isles, he had bought a mansion: the cargo, which he had taken months to collect, was to make it agreeable to Lydia's fastidious taste without spoiling its picturesque appearance. Plumbing and heating apparatus, building materials, some modern 'period' furniture. Only, the whole affair must be a surprise. The cargo which now lay in the sloping hold of the *Maggie* was more important than MacTaggart realised.

Wet to the knees, with the sand and water squelching to each step, Marshall pressed doggedly towards the shore. It was forty years or more since he had walked on a sandy beach, but he couldn't remember it being so wet or that there had been so much of it. Looking back he saw the *Maggie* as a small craft on the horizon, but the scrubby foreshore and the rising hills beyond seemed as far away as ever. He was breathing hard and perspiring. To lift each foot from the clinging sand was an effort. The Skipper, he noticed, was wearing Wellingtons and was so little exercised that he was puffing quite easily at his pipe.

Marshall said vindictively, 'I'll tell you something else. If you think that even if you did get away with that cargo, and landed it at Kiltarra, I'd pay you, you're out of your mind! You won't get another penny from me!'

The sand was drier near the shore, but, unexpectedly, as the beach ended, they came on a stretch of boggy ground. To Marshall this was even more of a hardship than the half-mile of sand, but the Skipper seemed so little concerned that he stopped to fill his pipe and was still only a few paces behind when they came at last to the road.

They strode silently along the quiet edges of the coast. It was a scene of utter tranquillity: the rising mountains, sheep grazing in the heather, a crofter's cottage in the sheltered lee of a quarry. The only human they saw on their long walk was a shepherd; the only sounds to break the mountain silence were the bleat of sheep and the occasional flutter of pheasants. At first Marshall led the way, striding along the rough road in an angry silence, but soon, as the stones began to cut through his thin city shoes, his pace flagged and he had difficulty in keeping up with the Skipper's unhurried step.

When they reached Loch Mora – two or three houses grouped round a pier and a stone wharf – the Skipper was still sauntering easily, but Marshall, some way behind, was a pathetic sight. He was out of condition and obviously in real pain. At the first of the houses the Skipper waited for him to limp up, but Marshall, staggering like a drunkard, passed him with a murderous look and made for the pub.

The innkeeper rose in some surprise as a man, apparently in the last stage of exhaustion, staggered through the doorway.

Marshall gasped, 'I'd like to use your . . . telephone.'

Chapter Seventeen

Campbell's voice came over the telephone with the air of incredulous amusement that Marshall had come to dread.

'On the beach, Mr Marshall? But how . . . ? The last time I heard from you . . .'

'We're on the beach,' Marshall insisted gratingly, 'What I want to know is, can your boat wait for us to get off?'

Campbell said, 'I'm afraid there's no possibility of keeping Captain Anderson's boat another day . . . no . . . I'm sorry.' He asked, 'Where are you, by the way?'

Marshall looked round as though he couldn't even be sure of this. The tiny bar, MacTaggart and the landlord talking closely, outside the blue water stretching away. 'I'm at a village – if you can call it that – called Loch Mora.'

Campbell's voice came, 'Well, if you'll hold on a minute, I'll just see . . .' He was back almost at once, 'By the way, our friend Fraser has been doing you well in the *Star*. You won't have seen it. "The Puffer. Marshall's Assistant on Charge".'

'One thing about you Scotsmen,' Marshall said, 'is your

wonderful sense of humour.' He asked plaintively, 'But what about Loch Mora?'

'Ah yes, Loch Mora. Well, you're in luck, Mr Marshall. We have a cattle boat calling there tomorrow afternoon to pick up some beasts. I've just checked in our records. There's an old abandoned pier which is being dismantled next week.'

Still holding the receiver, Marshall looked out of the window. There was a pier, undoubtedly: a rickety construction of wood which looked as though it might subside at any moment. 'Well,' Marshall said, 'It looks worse than abandoned. I'd say it was debauched.'

Campbell said, 'If ye can have your cargo there by three o'clock ready for loading I can put some stevedores aboard. But be sure to get your cargo on the wharf. The pier won't be strong enough to take it. The stevedores can manhandle the cargo out to the head of the pier, where our boat can load.' Suddenly he began to chuckle. 'I've just realised what you meant when you said that the pier looked worse than abandoned.' He laughed heartily. 'That's very amusing, Mr Marshall, very amusing. I must remember to tell Mrs Campbell.'

Marshall put his hand over his eyes. 'I'm simply full of witticisms today, Mr Campbell. I'm developing a comic temperament.' He went on briskly, 'Right, then, I'll see that . . . What? Three . . . Yes, just a moment, operator. Hold on.'

He searched, without much hope, through his pockets for some change, then, leaving the telephone, put a pound note on the bar. He said to the publican, 'Give me three shillings, will you?'

The publican raked through his till. 'Here ye are, sir.'

As Marshall walked back to the telephone he was half aware of the conversation between MacTaggart and the landlord and as he struggled to make the third, truly Scottish, shilling stay in the box he heard the gist of their conversation, accompanied every few seconds by the tin-tinnabulations of the reluctant shilling.

The landlord was saying, 'Have you heard about the celebration for Davie Macdougall, over at Bellabegwinnie?'

'Aye, it's wonderful to think of old Davie reaching his hundredth birthday.'

'There's a few people about was hoping to get over to Bellabegwinnie for the party. Will ye no' be going yeself, Peter?'

Marshall saw the Skipper look across speculatively, 'Hmm. I canna be sure.'

At last the box accepted the shilling and the line was open again to the CSS office at Glasgow. Marshall called, 'Hello, Mr Campbell.'

'Hallo. Can ye arrange all that, Mr Marshall?'

'I'll arrange it all right. The cargo will be sitting there on the wharf by three o'clock . . . Fine . . . Thank you very much.'

He replaced the receiver, and walked tiredly back to the bar to collect his change.

The Skipper looked at him hopefully. 'Would ye care for a wee drap a . . . ?'

He shook his head. 'No, thank you. Let's go. We may as well get back before dark.'

The Skipper suggested, 'Would ye no prefer to put up

here for the night? Ye'd be more comfortable, and we could bring the Puffer along first thing in the . . .'

Marshall moved wearily towards the door. 'Oh, *come on!*'

They trudged back along the torturing road. Marshall could hardly believe that feet could hurt so much or that shoes could prove so inadequate. He stumbled repeatedly, and once, for a few steps, he was glad to hold MacTaggart's arm.

When they reached the bay the tide was at half flood, and the *Maggie*, though still aground, was surrounded by water. Completely exhausted, Marshall sat on a rock while the Skipper signalled to his boat. In a few minutes the boy was rowing towards them in the dinghy.

When the Skipper shook his arm Marshall woke from the daze of exhaustion. 'The boat's here, sir. Ye'll have to wade.' Marshall looked up dumbly and saw the boy waiting in the dinghy, some fifty or sixty yards away. 'As close as he can get,' the Skipper shouted and started off through the shallow water in his Wellingtons.

Slowly, with immense care, Marshall unlaced and removed his shoes. Then he stumbled out behind the Skipper.

When he reached the dinghy he had no strength to climb over the side. He felt the Skipper's hand grasping his shoulder and the Skipper's cheerful voice, 'Weel, it's a grand evening. Do ye know, ye were right. The exercise has done me good.'

Chapter Eighteen

In his desperate tiredness Marshall slept longer and more soundly than he had for years. From the depths of slumber he had vague impressions, intangible as dreams, which, even on waking, could not be distinguished as fears or reality: the Skipper drinking, arguing lugubriously with the engineman; the boy's shrill defence of his hero; the mate's concertina; a rocking of the boat, rise and fall, the engine starting, the anchor chain . . .

Marshall woke slowly, and his eyes were open for a few seconds before he remembered where he was. Quite clearly above the noise of the engine he heard the sounds of movement. McGregor in his engine-room, the Skipper's voice, the cry of seagulls. He scrambled up, fully clothed except for his shoes and jacket, and tried to stand. His outraged feet were extremities of pain; his joints seemed to creak as loudly as the rotten timbers of the *Maggie*. He held himself upright against the bunk. A lesser man would have given up the fight, would have subsided despairingly into the blankets, but Marshall was a man of determination. He had to know what MacTaggart was doing. He had to know . . .

As he leant over the side of the bunk his head swam with fatigue. His shoes: one . . . two . . . Gritting his teeth he pressed first one foot into a shoe, then the other. Never again, he knew, would he buy shoes that were smart or tight-fitting. Brogues were the things, or Wellingtons. Hearing the Skipper's shout, 'Where's the wee boy?' he struggled to get on deck. One shoelace was fastened; the other broke under his impatient tugging. He stared at it furiously and then stuffed the broken end into his pocket.

Scrambling out of the hatch he saw that they were indeed under way. The sea was more choppy than yesterday, but the occasional whitecaps in the deep blueness of the sea added a touch of exhilaration to the scene. They also made the *Maggie* look faster than she was.

'Good morning, sir. It's a fine day.' Leaning from his wheelhouse the Skipper greeted him warmly, as though there had never been any misunderstanding about cargo, no chase, no hard words.

Marshall came fully out on to the sunlit deck and the fresh wind blowing his hair only added to the wildness of his appearance. 'Where are we? Where are we?'

The Skipper indicated with his pipe stem their position on the map. 'We'll be in Loch Mora under the hour, Mr Marshall. We're just about there. Ye can see Beinn Chareagach over yonder, and that's Beinn Na Croise on our port quarter.'

Despite the Skipper's fair words and open countenance Marshall would accept nothing on trust. He looked intently at the map, squinted suspiciously across the water to the line of mountains. He even took a compass bearing.

Unless the Skipper had produced a fake map they were, in fact, heading for Loch Mora. He could just see the dilapidated pier.

The boy came to his side. 'Will ye not be having some breakfast, sir?'

Marshall shook his head ungraciously. 'No, thanks. I'll wait till I get to . . .' He paused and his expression changed as he caught the odour from the galley. Yesterday's long walk and now the keen air, the sunlight, the scudding water. He hesitated, 'Well . . .'

In the forward cabin he attacked the plate of ham and eggs and the mug of tea set before him by the boy. As he ate he was aware that the boy, standing by the stove, was watching every mouthful.

'There's plenty more eggs, sir.'

'No, thanks.' Marshall cleaned the plate with a piece of bread and leaned back in his chair. 'Mmm . . . Mmm . . . That's the biggest meal I've eaten in years.'

The boy suggested eagerly, 'More tea?'

Marshall hesitated, then pushed the mug across. 'All right.' After the humdrum strain of business, the sudden apoplectic chase, he felt relaxed. In the untidy cabin, with the greasy plate, broken teapot, a mug of dark brown tea in his hand, it seemed impossible to judge things by any normal values. The Skipper was a rogue, but a cheerful rogue; the boy at least was loyal.

Marshall asked, 'Don't they ever call you anything but 'the wee boy'?'

'My name's Douggie, sir.' He had collected the plates, and was now washing them in a bucket of water.

Marshall said, 'Well, Douggie, you're a good ham and eggs cooker, anyway.'

From the smile that flickered across the pert, serious face it was obvious that the boy was pleased. For a few moments he washed with vigour, sloshing a good deal of water over the deck. Then he looked up. 'Why won't you let the Captain take the cargo for ye, Mr Marshall?'

Marshall was quite calm now. He explained reasonably and gently. 'Because he caused me a great deal of trouble and expense. You know that.'

'I know, sir. But why won't ye let him take the cargo for ye?'

'Well, he double-crossed me. He behaved very badly.'

'I know he did, sir. But why won't ye let him take the cargo for ye?'

Marshall drank his tea. He looked thoughtfully at the boy's serious face, then he chuckled and shook his head in admiration. He said, 'Douggie, I could use a few people like you in my own business. You'd better come and work for me.'

The boy considered this seriously. Then he explained, 'I wouldna want to leave the Captain, sir. The Captain is the best skipper in the coastal trade. Everybody knows that. There's not many skippers like Captain MacTaggart.'

Marshall subdued a smile. 'You're so right.' He leant forward. 'Tell me: was the Captain really born aboard this boat, or is that just a . . . ?'

The boy was collecting the knives and forks from the table. 'Yes, sir. He was. Right here in this cabin.'

'But how did that happen?'

'Well, sir. 'Twas like this. The *Maggie* was just launched then. The Captain's granddad was the skipper of her, and his dad was the mate. Well, the Captain was supposed to be born in Applecross, but his mother needed a doctor, so they were taking her across to Portree, and there was a storm . . .' He shrugged, 'So the Captain was born right here on the *Maggie*.'

Marshall was silent. He tried to imagine the rough night, the woman moaning in the bunk; the tossing boat, the husband at the wheel. And out of that night of agony had been born – the Skipper. He saw for the first time that under the bland air of untrustworthy innocence the Skipper really did love the *Maggie*. She was more to him than any other boat could ever be.

The boy was saying, 'If we got the rest of the money from ye, sir, we could get her plates put right. It would mean a lot to the Captain. Why won't ye let him take the cargo for ye, sir?'

Chapter Nineteen

(1)

In the morning sunlight Loch Mora looked picturesque but deserted: hardly the place for a swift movement of cargo. As the *Maggie* tied up at the wharf a crofter drove a few shaggy cattle out on to the dilapidated pier, where they stood looking disconsolately over the water. The pub door was shut, and only the lowing of a bull from some hidden barn showed that there was life at all in the cluster of cottages. The rising moorland was deserted, and along the line of hills a dark pine forest rose like a wall.

Marshall called to the crew, 'Come on now. Let's get moving. We'll be hard pushed as it is before the CSS boat comes in.'

The three men and the boy started reluctantly to unload the cargo, with McGregor controlling the donkey-engine and the mate at the derrick. The Skipper shuffled between the hold and the wharf, showing by his good example how to forgive a personal affront. The boy, following him backwards and forwards, looked so bitterly at Marshall that the American found himself turning away in embarrassment. Was he really to be blamed for wanting his cargo safe? Any rational observer would confirm that the old Puffer was unseaworthy. There were many hazards between Loch Mora and Kiltarra: rough seas, uncertain tides, rocky shores, where a boat could have the bottom ripped out of her in a matter of minutes. And was the Skipper such a good seaman that he could be trusted to deliver the cargo safely, whatever the hazards? Despite the boy's loyal protests Marshall could not forget the fiasco at Glasgow. 'Puffer stuck on subway!' And the pilot's admiring testimonial, 'I seen him so drunk . . . !'

Marshall shook away his doubts. 'Get a move on there. Get a move on!'

They worked stoically, accepting their fate – all except the Skipper. As the cargo piled on to the wharf he retreated to his wheelhouse, where he leant broodingly, looking at nothing and saying nothing, but, Marshall felt, thinking a lot. He would have given a great deal to have known what plans were hatching behind that formidable nose and the bright speculative eyes. Marshall moved uneasily along the wharf, trying to think what he would do if he were in MacTaggart's place. But it was no good. The man was a lunatic. Although he couldn't feel entirely at rest until the CSS boat came in, he could see no possible weakness that even a man of MacTaggart's ingenuity could turn to advantage. The cargo was there, on the stone wharf: the last crate was being landed.

He looked towards the pub. The door was open now and the landlord standing in the doorway raised a hand in salutation. There was a window facing the wharf. Marshall called, 'MacTaggart!'

'Aye?'

'I'm going over to the pub to phone. But, in case you should have any bright ideas, remember that I'll be by the window. I'll be able to see everything.'

(2)

The wee boy walked disconsolately along the deck. His face was dirty and his hands were cut from handling the wooden crates; but his physical discomfort was nothing compared with his soreness of spirit. The Skipper had been defeated. The *Maggie* would be sold or broken up. The inevitable end was near. He dragged wearily towards the stern.

Then he stopped. Here was something that no one had seen, not even Marshall. The rails at the stern were broken and the stern was projecting eighteen inches or so directly under the heavy cross-beams of the pier. As the *Maggie* rose with the tide . . . ! He turned excitedly to the wheel-house. 'Captain, sir!'

The Skipper turned disinterestedly, 'Aye?'

'Captain, sir, look at the way she's lying. When the tide comes in will she no' catch under the pier?'

The Skipper turned without undue concern. A foot or two in reverse. There was no hurry.

The boy said timorously, 'Wait a minute, sir . . . I mean, sir . . . If ye left her the way she is, and the tide comes in, would there no' be an . . . accident?'

At first the Skipper did not grasp the point. 'Are ye daft, lad? It would ruin . . .' His voice trailed off as understanding showed in his eyes. He looked guilelessly across at the pub where Marshall was telephoning by the open window. The American was watching alertly, but no one could see what was happening or what was likely to happen under the pier except from the deck of the *Maggie*. The Skipper smiled broadly as he clapped the wee boy on the shoulder. 'Aye,' he said. 'Just leave her the way she is. Ye're a good lad, Douggie. A good lad, and I'm not denying it. Ye'll be a skipper one day, yourself.'

(3)

Marshall could not have said how soon he began to sense that something was wrong. Along the window ledge beside the telephone he had placed neat stacks of shillings; the window was open and, as he had said, he could see everything that happened on the wharf. McGregor was there and Hamish the mate. The Skipper and the boy were talking on deck.

He started as the operator connected him with his number. 'Hallo, World International Airways?' Then for a few minutes his attention was diverted as a grubby boy came along the road, driving a score of geese. As they waddled across the cobbles they protested with waggling tails, outstretched necks and a loud indignant cackling. Auk-auk-auk! Auk-auk-auk! Marshall looked furiously at the urchin and then at the crew, who were watching him with amusement from the wharf. He dared not shut the window. It even crossed his mind that they might have arranged this – as a diversion? It could easily be the fruit of MacTaggart's fertile brain. Auk–auk–auk!

'Hallo! World International . . . ? Hallo!'

He put down the receiver and slammed the door shut.

'Hallo! Hallo! Is that . . . ?' He bellowed angrily. 'Who's shouting? Do you know who you're talking to?' Down the road the cackling came as mocking laughter. Auk–auk–auk! Auk–auk–auk!

His piles of shillings diminished as he indulged in an orgy of telephoning: so many orders to be given, so much to arrange. And on the wharf the Skipper and boy had joined McGregor and the mate. They were laughing uproariously together. Was it then that he had his first premonition of disaster?

He hurried through his last conversation. 'Right. Thank you, Miss Peters. Tell Mrs Marshall I will definitely be home tomorrow. Thank you.' He replaced the receiver slowly as the *Maggie*'s crew came across the sunlit road. He heard the Skipper's cheerful cry, 'All right, lads, I'll buy the drinks.'

Marshall took a few paces into the road and then stopped to watch as they approached. His misgivings grew as they came nearer. They were laughing, nudging, full of the joys of life, such an extraordinary change of attitude from their previous despondency.

They passed close to him without stopping. They were all grinning fatuously and, as they entered the pub, the mate began to giggle. Marshall turned and followed them into the bar.

He stood aggressively in the doorway. 'All right, all right. Let me in on it, will you? What's so funny?'

They turned together, leaning on the bar, and looked at him with bland innocence.

'Oh, hell!' Marshall stalked angrily into the road and crossed over to the wharf.

His first thoughts were for his cargo. Crates, timber, machinery: he checked it all carefully, pressing his finger into sacking covers, testing the weight of boxed crates. There was nothing wrong that he could see. He sat down on guard. Far out on the water a cargo boat was turning shorewards. The CSS boat? A surge of laughter came from the pub, across the deserted street, and up into the silent hills. A dog was sniffing round the cargo. At the end of the pier the cattle bellowed mournfully to the sea. Marshall sat doggedly on guard.

Although there was no possibility of disaster that he could see, he still turned uneasily from the merriment in the pub. A piano was played for a few inaccurate bars. Outside in the sunlight the boy was staring over the sea. Marshall tried to laugh away his fears: the cargo was here, on the wharf; he was sitting on it. The CSS boat was on its way.

One of the cattle lowed and was answered by its mate. Then again . . . Marshall looked round, puzzled. It seemed to him that the sound he had just heard, a deep, hoarse groaning, had not come from the cattle. And yet . . . He couldn't be sure. It was like the lowing he had heard before and yet, somehow, different. Perhaps he had been mistaken.

He settled down again, and again the noise broke through his complacency. There was no doubt about it this time. It hadn't come from the cattle. He saw them standing dejectedly with heads bent, silent. The deep groaning came again.

Marshall turned curiously but without much alarm to the pier. It *must* be the cattle! He walked out, picking his way carefully across the rotten timbers, until he was standing only a few yards from the end of the pier. Now then! The noise was repeated, more loudly than before, and it was now behind him, between the pier and the wharf.

He looked suspiciously round but could find nothing to account for the noise. Outside the pub the boy was standing up and the three senior members of the crew had come to the open window with beer glasses in their hands. Marshall began to panic.

The groaning was almost continuous now although it seemed to increase and lessen in intensity with the ebb and flow of each wave. The pier! He could feel the whole framework shuddering. The warning sounds were now deep and nerve-shattering. The timbers beneath his feet were bending and groaning. Rise and fall; screech, shudder. Utterly bewildered, he tried desperately to remain calm. He couldn't understand what was happening.

Then, abruptly, one of the cross-planks of the pier tore loose from its beam and sprang into the air. Marshall turned in panic.

'Hey!'

He called desperately to the *Maggie*'s crew, and at that moment realised what had happened.

'Hey!'

The stern of the Puffer was lifting one of the big cross-timbers from the top of the vertical piles. Marshall, on the jetty beyond, felt the whole structure heaving beneath his feet. Two more boards sprang loose. Shouting wildly he raced towards the stone wharf and the pub.

'Hey! Hey!'

As he dashed across the road the Skipper, the engine-man and the mate turned quickly back to the bar. He rushed through the open doorway, shouting, 'Hey! Move that boat! It's breaking up the pier!'

The Skipper turned with one elbow on the bar. He seemed astonished. 'What?'

Marshall could not wait for any subtle acting. He seized the Skipper by the arm and propelled him towards the door. 'Hurry up, will you? It's stuck under the timbers!'

'Stuck under the timbers!'

Marshall dashed back towards the wharf, followed at an ambling trot by the Skipper, the engineman, the mate and the wee boy.

The pier was now screaming like a hundred souls in torment. The woodwork was moving with the undulations of a gentle earthquake. Marshall stared down at the stern of the *Maggie*, which was supporting the full weight of the beam and had lifted it several inches into the air. He gesticulated at the Skipper and shouted above the screeching timbers, 'Move it! Get it out of there!'

The Skipper asked cautiously, 'Don't ye think, sir, t'would be better, all things considered, if you'll pardon . . .'

'Don't stand there, you old fool!'

With a shrug the Skipper climbed aboard the *Maggie*. He went into the wheelhouse and beckoned to McGregor.

Like a demented man Marshall rushed out on to the pier. He leant over to inspect the damage. 'Hurry up, will you? Get it out of here!'

The Skipper gave, 'Full steam ahead.'

For a moment nothing moved. The waters churned madly, the *Maggie* strained, the pier resisted with even more ominous sounds of rending timbers.

Then, slowly, the *Maggie* began to move forward. As it pushed inch by inch into the deeper water it carried the massive pier timber sideways, out from its seating, away from the vertical piles. The lateral planks splayed upwards like the keys of a broken piano. Marshall watched, aghast, and scampered out to the end of the pier.

He stood among the passive cattle and saw the hideous destruction: tearing planks, swaying timbers. He shouted above the din, 'Go back! Go back!' He saw the Skipper cup his ear and bend enquiringly towards the engineman.

'Go back! Go back!'

The Skipper shrugged and with the engineman's help pushed over the big lever to put the Puffer into reverse.

Having won the mighty tug-of-war, the *Maggie* now pushed gamely in reverse. For a moment she could make no sternway. Her propeller thrashed the water, the pier resisted. Then slowly she began to move. Pushing the timbers which had become dislodged, she suddenly created worse damage by forcing some lateral bars to dislodge the beam on the far side. The beam collapsed suddenly, and the Puffer charged backwards into the pier. The whole structure crumbled under the onslaught.

Marshall was caught unawares by the sudden collapse. He leaped to safety at the very end of the pier and then, turning in panic, screamed hoarsely, 'No! No! The other way!'

The Skipper and McGregor looked at each other and then at Marshall. Theirs not to reason why! They put the Puffer into forward gear again.

As the *Maggie* pulled out, a worthy victor, she took with her most of the broken timbers of the pier. The large beam and an assortment of planks lay across her stern. As she pulled clear of the débris the rest of the jetty collapsed, sinking gracefully into the sea and leaving a clear gap of water between Marshall and the wharf.

'Holy smoke!' Standing, dazed and distraught, on his little island of wood, with the shaggy cattle looking mournfully at the damage, Marshall seemed too upset to move. He stared with a sort of horrified disbelief at the gap of water, the few floating timbers, the *Maggie* pulling discreetly out of earshot. But he was too stunned to shout, too bewildered for anger.

A ship's hooter sounded behind him. The CSS boat was coming at half-speed towards what remained of the pier. He heard the captain shout to one of his seamen, 'Ach, will ye look at that! MacTaggart's surpassed himself wi' this.'

The cargo vessel was alongside. A seaman leapt on to the pier, causing a minor stir among the cattle. A gangplank was lowered. Someone – the captain – was coming ashore. All of these movements registered in Marshall's brain without causing him to turn. He was staring at the old Puffer, which, seeing that there was to be no immediate bloodshed, was sidling back to the wharf.

The CSS captain came respectfully, commiseratingly, to Marshall's shoulder.

'Are you Mr Marshall, sir?'

Still staring at the Puffer, Marshall answered slowly, 'Well, I'm no longer absolutely sure.'

The captain said apologetically, 'I'm afraid there's nothing we can do for you, sir. We can't get your cargo out here and we draw too much to put in by the wharf.'

'I know.'

The captain moved awkwardly away. 'You realise . . . There's nothing can get to it but a Puffer.' He touched his cap. 'Well . . . good day to you, sir.'

Marshall slumped dispiritedly on a bollard while the cattle were driven on to the boat. He heard the gangplank being drawn up, the engine-room bell ringing. Without turning his head he knew that the boat which was to have been his salvation was pulling out into deep water, and that he was alone in his dejection. He sat with his chin resting in the palm of one hand. His thoughts turned introspectively to his own part in the sad affair. Could he have foreseen all that had happened? Would he have been tricked like this ten, twenty years ago? He wondered gloomily whether he was growing old. But common sense told him that you didn't meet a lunatic genius every day of the week: once in a lifetime – if you were unlucky! The thing now was to cut his losses.

Something bumped against the other side of the pier-head. He rose calmly enough and looked down at the wee boy, who was waiting with shipped oars in the dinghy. The small boat rose and fell, rose and fell, against the timber like a cat rubbing ingratiatingly against a trouser leg. The boy looked up without speaking, but obviously inviting the American to descend. Marshall rubbed his hands across his face, as though he could wipe out the angry thoughts. Then as he looked down expressively the boy reached up to him and smiled.

He climbed, a beaten man, on to the wharf and slouched despondently across the road. In the pub the Skipper and crew of the *Maggie* eyed him uneasily. They leant against the bar with newly filled pint pots and watched him slump on one of the benches.

The Skipper said understandingly, 'Aye, it's a bad business, sir, a bad business. I'm right sorry for ye, Mr Marshall.' He waited cautiously and then waved his hand towards the array of bottles. 'Can I get ye a wee drap . . . ?'

'No, thanks.'

For a few uneasy minutes they drank in silence. The American still seemed like a man in a dream. The Skipper cleared his throat. 'Of course, it's not what ye wanted, Mr Marshall, but there's no need for ye to worry unduly. Maybe the CSS boat couldn't help ye, but there's always the auld *Maggie*. We'll be glad to help ye out.'

'I know.'

The Skipper seemed to be content to leave the matter there until McGregor nudged him back to the attack. He rubbed his hand over his beard. 'Of course, ye understand,

Mr Marshall, I have every sympathy for ye in your predicament. But it wouldna be in our best interests to take the job unless it was for the whole journey to Kiltarra . . .' He hesitated as Marshall slowly raised his head '. . . and without meaning any offence, of course, it would simplify matters if you could see your way to letting us have the rest of our fee in advance.'

Marshall stared at him for a full minute without speaking. Then, without a word, he took out his cheque-book and fountain pen.

The Skipper turned with relief to the landlord. 'Ah weel, John, ye'd better set them up again.'

Chapter Twenty

It seemed to Marshall that the village, which only an hour ago had seemed almost devoid of life, was now bustling with activity. MacTaggart and his crew were working with an efficiency he would not have thought possible. The donkey-engine whirled, the derrick swung. Hooks grappled, the ropes tautened. With an unbelievable swiftness the pile of cargo on the wharf diminished until there were only two crates, a length of timber.

As the last crate was lifted Marshall saw a small gathering of villagers on the wharf. They were dressed for travelling and their luggage lay in a neat pile approximately where his own cargo had lain. He saw two suitcases, several boxes and some small crates containing ducks, a pair of geese, three young pigs and a turkey. Probably waiting for the bus, he thought, forgetting that the road he had walked along so painfully last evening was too rocky, too boggy, too pot-holed for any bus.

He forgot about them as he turned to the telephone. With a fresh stack of shillings he tried once again to contact his own efficient world. By the time he had been connected with Glasgow and then with London he was even more dejected than before. He hung up the receiver and walked heavily to the door.

The group of villagers had gone with their baggage, and as he walked across the wharf the mate and the wee boy started to cast off. He climbed aboard the *Maggie* and walked to his lonely position in the stern. As the Puffer began to slide away from the wharf the mate and the boy leapt on board. The Skipper signalled 'Full speed' and they moved smoothly out into the open sea.

It was a grand day. The sun was high in the heavens now. The cottages of Loch Mora, the broken pier, the white road leading over the hill, dwindled and merged into the rising greenness of the mountain. The engines thumped steadily, a cohort of seagulls glided effortlessly over their wake.

It was not long before the Skipper noticed that Marshall was not appreciating the beauty of the day. He called back, 'Anything wrong, Mr Marshall?'

Marshall said, 'You'll probably be amused to hear that Pusey is now out of jail.'

The Skipper nodded. 'Ach, aye. That's good news, sir. I was very disturbed by that unfortunate . . .'

Marshall walked past him to the hatch of the captain's cabin. He paused at the top of the ladder and said bleakly, 'And you'll probably be equally amused when I tell you that my wife's found out about what I'm doing, which is the one thing I didn't want to happen.' He went down the hatch, leaving the Skipper and the engineman mystified and rather concerned.

Down in the cabin Marshall tried to work. He had some papers spread across the table, a schedule of accounts. But he couldn't concentrate. He was like a gambler who had lost so heavily that caution seemed an unnecessary frustration. Time, time, time: he couldn't – wouldn't – calculate how much of it he had lost. Away on this nightmare adventure; Pusey in prison, Lydia restlessly probing; he wondered what sort of world he would return to if ever he succeeded in reaching Kiltarra.

He rose and walked restlessly to the broken mirror. The stubbled, worried, unconfident face that confronted him was not the face of Calvin B. Marshall. Would he ever look the same again? He stuck out his jaw. At least he could try.

As he climbed out of the hatch on to the deck he saw the Skipper watching him nervously from the wheelhouse. Marshall said, 'I need a shave. Do you think you could lend me . . .' He stopped and turned in amazement as a pig squealed loudly. He couldn't believe it.

On the deck near the bows lay the baggage he had seen on the wharf: the suitcases, the boxes, the crates of ducks and geese and pigs, a young turkey. He walked slowly across. His amazement was suddenly increased by the appearance of a child from behind the mast.

'What the . . . !' He looked up at the Skipper and then stopped in further surprise.

Beside the wheelhouse, opposite the hatch, the villagers he had seen on the wharf were sitting and chatting with the crew. There were three men, two women, a young girl and the child. They were looking at him with interest and curiosity.

As Marshall turned speechlessly towards the wheelhouse the Skipper handed over the wheel to the mate and walked down to the deck.

'They were wanting a lift, sir. I thought ye would not mind if we dropped them off on the way.' He turned and beckoned to the strangers, who came forward smiling affably. The first man held out his hand. The Skipper said, 'Mr Marshall, Mr Macdougall.'

Still bewildered, Marshall greeted, 'How do you do, Mr Macdougall?' He looked up at the sun. 'South! Why are we sailing south?'

The Skipper explained, 'We have to take on some coal at Bellabegwinnie'; and then, quickly, 'Mr Marshall, Mr Roger Macdougall.'

Marshall shook hands again. 'How are you?' He still could orientate himself. 'But isn't that out of our way?'

'Just a bit, sir, but it'll . . .' The Skipper beckoned one of the ladies. 'Mrs Macdougall, Mr Marshall, the owner of our cargo. It will save us time in the end, sir.' He presented the girl. 'Miss Macdougall, this is Mr Marshall.'

Refusing to panic, Marshall managed to force a smile. 'How do you do?'

Bellabegwinnie seemed even smaller, even more remote, than Loch Mora. Lining the harbour were a few houses, a tiny pub; not even a chapel. But despite its smallness there seemed to be quite a number of Bellabegwinnians moving about the pier and the front. The small harbour was crowded with other craft, another Puffer, a trawler, and several ring-net fishing boats. Standing in the bows Marshall noted their presence, and no more: he was past surprises. There comes a time in every period of suffering when the spirit turns from the thought of more pain. The mind goes stoically blank. Nothing matters any more: nothing. Marshall had reached this point.

As the *Maggie* edged carefully between the litter of craft he didn't try to reason what it was all about. Fingering his clean-shaven jowls, the patch of plaster on his chin, he waited for what fate would bring.

It brought a friendly, humorous crowd of Bellabegwinnians, who waved, shouted, helped to secure the ropes. They seemed genuinely glad to see MacTaggart and his crew.

Marshall climbed up on to the pier. He said, 'I have an important call to make and I want to buy a change of clothes. Have we time for that?'

The Skipper waved generously. 'Oh, I think we might manage that, sir.'

Marshall nodded, looked round at the gathering of boats, the unexpected crowd; but catching the Skipper's bland expression he turned towards the cottages. He wasn't going to reason things out. He wasn't going to worry.

There was more to the village than he had supposed. Round a shoulder of the hill there was a cluster of houses, a chapel, another pub. He even found a general stores. He looked at the goods in the window: fishing tackle, lead weights, paternosters, breakfast cereals, a side of bacon; children's bonnets, a lady's dress, Wellingtons; brooms, shovels, a dustbin; a birdcage, flypaper, scouring powder. The door-bell pinged as he walked diffidently in.

'Gude day, sir.'

'Oh . . . good day. I wonder . . .' He looked round in embarrassment and caught the interested gaze of two old women, a girl and a small boy who were waiting to be served.

'Yes?'

'I wonder . . .' He felt the colour mounting on his neck. 'What I really want is some clothes.'

'Clothes, sir?'

'Yes.' He asked. 'You do sell clothes?'

'Oh, aye. What sort of clothes would ye be wanting?'

'Well . . .' He gestured vaguely, like an unconfident actor before a critical audience. 'Some trousers, some . . .' He explained, 'I want something a bit more suitable for sailing.'

The lady behind the counter looked at his good city suit, now sadly stained and creased, his crumpled shirt and collar. She agreed, 'Ye certainly want a change. Would ye care to go through to the parlour?' She opened the inner door and shouted, 'Jamie, here's a gentleman wants some trews!'

Later − much later, it seemed − he stepped self-consciously out into the village street. A heavy turtle-neck sweater, dungarees, and seamen's boots. He was dreading the moment when the *Maggie*'s crew would see him first. He stopped a boy who was wobbling precariously past on a ramshackle bicycle.

'Can you direct me to the post office?'

'Eh?'

'Can you direct me to the post office?'

The boy stared at him as though he were mad. He pointed at the general stores. 'Yon's the post office.'

Gathering the scattered threads of confidence he went back to the door. Ping! The shoppers, who had obviously been discussing him with relish, stared in fresh surprise. He went in, forgetting the step, and stumbled until his arms embraced a stout lady with a shopping bag.

'I do beg your pardon, madam!'

She watched with astonishment as he backed away between the boxes of oatmeal and potatoes. A saucepan clattered across the stone floor. He asked miserably, 'Is this the post office?'

'Aye.'

'Could I, do you think . . . ? Do you think I could use your telephone?'

Obviously suspicious of his extraordinary conduct the shop lady said grimly, 'If ye pay for it.'

'Of course.' He went into the small inner room. The telephone . . . ? He couldn't see at first in the gloom. Then, as he lifted the receiver, 'I want . . .' He paused, with another attack of cold fear. 'One moment, please.' He put down the receiver.

'Number, please?'

He fumbled through his trousers pockets: two pennies, a Scottish sixpence, bent beyond recall. Hurriedly he felt for his waistcoat, but it was hidden now beneath the sweater.

'What number would ye be wanting?'

He shouted desperately, 'One moment. I shan't keep you . . . Just got to get some change . . .'

He went back into the shop like a demented man. From their guarded looks and the way they backed into safer positions behind barrels or the counter it was plain that they had heard everything. They were convinced that he was a lunatic.

He calmed himself with an effort. 'Do you think you could let me have some change?'

The lady behind the counter watched him open-mouthed.

He repeated, 'Do you think you could let me have some change?'

'Change?'

'Change!' He felt his control slipping. 'Shillings, sixpennies, pennies! I-want-some-change-for-the-telephone.'

With his cupped hands brimming over with money he stamped irascibly back to the telephone.

'Hallo, hallo! You there, miss . . .'

The refined voice chided him gently, 'What number would ye be wanting?'

Chapter Twenty-One

All his anger and impatience wilted in the stuffy twilight of the post office. In a few minutes he was forcing polite words between his teeth; after the half-hour he was pleading, 'Miss, do you think . . . ? Could you try again?' He could see the elderly shopkeeper listening with disapproval.

'Hallo, Lydia!' His cry of relief was instantly muted to his wife's protest. 'But, honey, I didn't mean to shout. It's just that I'm so glad to hear you . . . Yes, I know . . . Yes, but honestly, honey, it's not been my fault . . . I know I promised . . . I really thought . . . If you could only see the man I've had to deal with.'

His head bowed, his eyes closed, as the last sediment of confidence drained away. 'Yes, honey . . . Yes, honey . . . Yes, honey, of course I'm still manager . . . Yes, honey . . . But this man MacTaggart . . . Yes, honey . . . I'm sorry, honey . . .'

His body sagged with his hopes, first one elbow against the telephone bracket, then leaning against the wall, half kneeling in supplication.

'But, Lydia, how can you say it's a silly idea when you haven't even seen the place? I promise you you'll absolutely love it! It's beautiful, Lydia, believe me. And we'll be able to spend most of the summers there . . . what? Of *course* I'll be there with you . . . But, honey, I've only gone to all this trouble because I wanted to make you happy . . . You're *what*? But you can't do that! No, we can't talk about it like this, over the phone. Look, darling, will you do something for me? I want you to fly out to Kiltarra. We'll be there some time in the late afternoon, and then we can sit down and discuss it reasonably . . . Hello? Hello, operator! Operator, we've been cut off! Operator!'

The operator's voice came gently, 'Your party's no longer there, sir.'

He nodded. 'Thank you. Thank you.'

He hung the receiver back on its hook. Then for a moment he stood quite still, like someone who has suffered an unexpected shock. He turned, staring vacantly at the postmistress. 'Uh – thank you. Thank you.'

Out in the village street he stood undecided. A quarter of a mile to the boat, in these clothes! The other way, where the mountain almost swept the coast road into the sea, would be quieter. He wanted time to think. At the end of the village the cobbles gave way to sand, and the sand petered out into heather: a few rabbit tracks, a sheep walk, a path beaten out of the hillside by generations of lovers. He wandered aimlessly, climbing wherever the myriad paths led, until he sank exhausted on to a mound of short grass. Looking down, he could see the jagged coastline, the bays, the beaches, the rocks, to the end of a promontory which jutted a mile or so away into the grey Atlantic. Below him, the road came from nowhere into the first houses of the village. The sharp roofs, the square chapel, the stores: he could just see round a buttress of the hill to the harbour where a dozen small boats were at anchor. His cargo! The momentary qualm faded as quickly as it came. What did it matter? If MacTaggart sailed off, if the *Maggie* sank . . . Now that he had no need to worry he looked back incredulously at his ferocious efforts over the last days: chartered planes, hectic phone calls, lawyers, hired cars, stacks of shillings! For all Lydia cared . . .

He turned from his introspection as he saw someone coming towards him through the heather. At first, when she was some way off, he thought she was just a child, but as she approached, swinging her legs youthfully against the heather, he saw that she was older than he had thought: nineteen or twenty, he guessed, and as pretty as a picture.

She was coming downhill, making for the village, but when she saw him she turned and came along the path towards him.

'Good afternoon.' He rose awkwardly, feeling embarrassed and yet, somehow, exhilarated by her young smiling face.

She asked, 'Would you be the American that came on Skipper MacTaggart's old Puffer?'

'That's right.'

She stared at him with the bright-eyed inquisitiveness of a child. 'I'm glad to have met ye. They told me ye'd want to be leaving soon. I'd have been sorry if ye'd left before I saw you.'

He walked beside her down the gradual slope. 'Why did you want to see me?' with a laugh. 'I can't be as famous as all that.'

She looked at him seriously. 'Famous? It's not that. It's just . . . I've never seen an American before.'

They walked down to the level track into the village, and, listening to her gay chatter, Marshall felt his depression lifting. For the second time that day he had to adjust his sense of proportion. She was youth and happiness and laughter; she was hope; she was life. Remembering his own young wife, he felt courage to continue the fight. Kiltarra. With the cargo he had collected so carefully, the cargo that was still in the *Maggie*'s hold . . .

The *Maggie*! Was she still there? Was MacTaggart waiting? He turned to the girl, 'Well, Miss, it sure has been nice meeting you.'

'It was nice to meet you, too.'

'Thank you.' He hesitated. 'Do you mind . . . ? Will you tell me your name?'

'Sheena,' she answered without embarrassment. 'What's yours?'

'Marshall'; he added self-consciously, 'Calvin B. Marshall.'

He hurried along the street, past the stores and the chapel, the second pub. His spirits were high again. He would carry out his original plan. First, to get his cargo to Kiltarra . . .

As he came round the bend of the hill he expected to see the *Maggie* with steam up and the crew waiting anxiously to cast off. But the boat was empty. Had they gone into the village looking for him? He was almost up to the.

boat before he saw the *Maggie* was not quite deserted. The wee boy was on hands and knees, scrubbing down the deck.

Marshall stopped by the ladder and looked round. He asked, 'Where are the others?'

With a faint but unmistakable air of guilt the boy said, 'In the village, sir.'

'But aren't we ready to go?' He looked round. 'Have they taken on the coal?'

'Well, no, sir . . .'

Marshall could feel exasperation rising again. A few minutes ago he had been ready to forget and forgive. Now . . . He asked angrily, 'What exactly is going on here?'

'They'll just be down in the village, sir.'

Two fishermen from one of the other boats were walking along the pier. They called to the boy, 'Hallo, Douggie. Have ye come for Dave Macdougall's party?'

Slowly, as he saw the boy's embarrassment, Marshall understood. He had been tricked again. With an expression of ferocious resolve he started down the road to the village.

Chapter Twenty-Two

As he strode up the cobbled hill he could see the Skipper through the open doorway of the pub. With a pint pot held affectionately in one hand MacTaggart was talking with four or five old friends, seafaring men like himself. Marshall saw him empty a glass with one long draught and accept another. He was saying, 'We'll have to bring Mr Marshall to the party. I'd like him to meet old Davie.'

Marshall put his head in the doorway and called quietly, 'MacTaggart!'

The Skipper looked round with an affable smile. 'Ah, Mr Marshall. I was just coming to find ye.' He seemed taken aback by Marshall's impatient gesture, and followed him a little nervously into the street. 'They canna let us have the coal before tomorrow . . .'

Calmly, wearily, the American sat on a bench outside the door and pulled the Skipper down beside him. He said carefully, 'Look, MacTaggart. I know you came here because somebody's having a party. I just want to ask you one thing . . .'

'Well, it's old Davie Macdougall, sir. He sailed with . . .'

'I know. He sailed with your father. So okay. I just want to ask you one thing.'

'Not my father, sir, my grandfather, Old Davie was mate when the *Maggie* was new.'

Marshall's voice rose with exasperation. 'All right, all right. I still want to ask you one thing. Doesn't the job you're supposed to be doing mean anything to you at all?'

'It means a great deal, sir,' the Skipper protested. 'Aye, we'll be able to get the *Maggie*'s plates put right. I'm very grateful to ye for the opportunity.'

'But don't you think you ought to fulfil your contract?'

The Skipper looked at him in surprise. 'What contract, sir?'

'You're supposed to be taking me and my cargo to Kiltarra!'

'But we are taking ye, sir. Ye're almost there. It's only one day's sailing. If we're away first thing in the morning . . .'

Marshall spoke with emotion. 'Listen, MacTaggart. You forced me into paying you in advance when you broke up that pier . . .'

'Forced ye, sir?' The Skipper was scandalised. 'Ye canna say we forced ye. Your cargo was practically stranded.'

'MacTaggart, don't you realise that if you fail to keep your bargain I can stop payment of the cheque I gave you?'

The threat had no effect at all. The Skipper said cheerfully, 'Och, no. Ye couldna do that, Mr Marshall.'

'No?' The American eyed him narrowly. 'If you don't come down there and get that thing under way right now . . .'

'Ye couldna refuse to pay us.'

The Skipper's grin infuriated Marshall beyond control. He shouted, '*Why* couldn't I? Why *can't* I? Why *wouldn't* I?'

The Skipper said confidently, 'Ach, because ye're an honourable man, Mr Marshall. I recognised ye for an honourable man the first minute I saw ye.'

'But, MacTaggart . . .'

'Ye've nothing to worry about, sir,' the Skipper said, clapping him on the shoulder. 'We'll get ye there. And, Mr Marshall, I've been instructed to tell ye that ye're included in the invitations to the party. It'll be a grand gathering, sir.'

The American rose in frustration, stared at him speechlessly for a moment, and walked furiously back towards the harbour.

The scene was darkening as he came slowly towards the old Puffer. There was a haze over the sea and the horizon was shortening as night fell. The boats rode quietly at anchor, and the line of hills was marked against a red sky.

As he climbed on to the deck Marshall felt something more than anger – an almost unbearable loneliness. The harbour was deserted. The boats were unmanned, the fishermen's nets were folded. Where he might have expected to see men pushing the smooth-running keels over the stones there was nothing except a few lobster pots, a meditating seagull. Everyone had gone to the party: everyone.

He went down into the cabin and lay despondently on the bunk. Courage and hope were seeping away in the lonely night. He felt cold and tired and disillusioned. Faintly, above the quiet harbour noises, came a distant chorus and a concertina. For a time he listened restlessly and then, swinging out of the bunk, made his way on to the deck.

When he went to the stern rail the sound of music was much louder. In a brightly lit hall, only a few hundred yards away, a dozen voices were lifted in a Gaelic song. Everyone in Bellabegwinnie seemed to be at the celebration. The joyful music had a melancholy ring for the American, leaning first on the rail, then against the wheelhouse door. His thoughts were at Kiltarra with the house he had planned, in London with the lovely, impatient Lydia, on the hillside with the girl Sheena.

Suddenly he was conscious of a heightening of tempo in the celebration hall. The first few voices were joined by many others as all the villagers and their guests roared into a Gaelic song. Marshall listened intently.

Then, as suddenly as it had arisen, the storm of singing died down. There was complete silence. On a sudden impulse Marshall climbed on to the pier and walked slowly towards the hall. He came quietly to one of the open windows and looked in.

There were nearly a hundred people in the hall, which was clearly a schoolroom converted for the party. They were all dressed in their best clothes. At one end of the room, on the teacher's dais, Davie Macdougall was sitting in the place of honour. He was a fine-looking man, upright, smiling, bright-eyed. Sometimes singly, sometimes in pairs, sometimes in small family groups the villagers and their guests went forward with their presents: geese, pheasants, pigs, sweaters, pipes, a sizeable keg. Round the old man's chair the pile of presents grew as each donor came forward to shake his hand or, if the donor was a lady, to kiss his cheek. Davie Macdougall was smiling broadly despite his tears.

Watching from the dark loneliness beyond the window Marshall felt strangely touched by what he had seen. There was friendship here and warmth, a charming sincerity that was not often met in his own efficient world of finance.

Only a few more gifts had to be presented. He saw the girl, Sheena, at the end of the line. Then, unexpectedly, the wee boy looked up and saw him standing at the window. Marshall took a step backwards, hoping to slip away into the darkness, but the boy had tugged at the Skipper's sleeve and the Skipper had started for the door.

He came out before Marshall could escape from the reflected light beyond the windows. He called, 'Mr Marshall! Mr Marshall! Won't ye come in and join us?'

Marshall's desire for flight was frustrated by MacTaggart's swiftness. Everyone in the hall had stopped at the interruption. As the light flooded through the open doorway the American was caught undecided. 'Come along, sir.' The Skipper had taken his arm.

Marshall shook his head in embarrassment. 'I'm sorry. I . . .'

The Skipper said, as he tugged him towards the doorway, 'But ye must come in, sir. Ye must meet Davie Macdougall.'

'Well . . .' Feeling more embarrassed with each reluctant step, Marshall allowed himself to be dragged into the room. The guests smiled politely. The engineman, the mate and the boy were plainly delighted. The Skipper led his passenger up to the old man. He said in Gaelic, 'Davie, this is Mr Marshall, a very important gentleman from America for whom we are doing a job. A fine man, Davie.' He said to Marshall, 'Shake hands with him, sir.'

Marshall took Davie Macdougall's hand in his own. The old man seemed to look him up and down, to size him up, and then, accepting him, returned his firm hand-clasp. Marshall said with an odd, sincere gesture, 'I haven't any . . . I haven't brought you a present . . .'

In Gaelic the Skipper said, 'Mr Marshall's concerned because he's brought no gift for you.'

Davie Macdougall smiled broadly and shook his head. Behind the wrinkled, weather-beaten skin his bright eyes showed only friendship.

Marshall said, 'Congratulations, sir,' and then, clumsily to the Skipper, 'Will you tell him that where I come from we have a saying that the first hundred years are the hardest.'

The Skipper nodded with quick approval. He translated, 'Mr Marshall asks me to tell ye that in America they have a saying, the first century is more difficult.'

The guests waited on tenterhooks to see whether the old man would take the joke. He said, 'I don't understand.'

The Skipper said again, 'The first century is more difficult than the second century.'

The room waited in silence. Somewhere a boy shuffled. 'Mother, why . . .?' and was instantly subdued. Davie Macdougall looked at Marshall seriously for a long minute as he considered the statement. Then suddenly his face was wreathed in smiles and he began to laugh. Marshall relaxed, and laughed with him. The whole room seemed pleased and relieved. The Skipper and the other guests joined in the laughter, some of them applauded the remark. The old man leant forward and took Marshall's hand again, and at once the musicians struck up with a dance. Following the Skipper across to the refreshment table Marshall felt inordinately pleased. He had come here a stranger. He had been accepted.

As he stood, smiling and watching the guests lining up for the dance, he felt a glass being pushed into his hand.

The Skipper said, 'Ye must have a wee dram in . . .'

Marshall shook his head doubtfully, anxious to avoid offence. 'No, thank you. I never take whisky.'

'In honour of the occasion, sir. Ye must.' He found himself ringed by the engineman, the mate and the boy. They were all grinning encouragement. 'No.' He tried to protest again, but he was hemmed in. There was nowhere to put the glass. 'Ye must, sir. In honour of . . .' With a fine feeling of bravado he swallowed the contents of the glass.

He coughed slightly and looked at them in surprise. 'Is that whisky?'

The Skipper said, 'Ach, not the kind ye're used to, sir. It's the old *uisge-beatha*. The water of life. Here, ye must have another, it'll give ye the mood for the dancing.'

Marshall started to protest again, but there was a lot of noise now and he could scarcely make himself heard. Fiddle, drums, concertina, stamping feet, whirling laughter, sudden screams of excitement. It was impossible to remain indifferent to the crescendo of gaiety. Stamp-beat-stamp: stamp-beat-stamp. He stood, grinning with pleasure, and he was not really surprised when he felt a touch on his arm and turned to face the girl Sheena. She stood before him, young and beautiful, and, with a gay directness, held out her hands to him for a dance. It was all part of the evening. Again Marshall protested, although not too vehemently, and he was not really upset when the engineman gave him a gentle push into the girl's arms.

With her cool hands gripping firmly she pulled him out on to the floor. For a second he panicked, realising that he knew nothing of their dance, not a single step, but as the girl seemed full of confidence he stayed. Very awkwardly at first, and with his eyes watching every movement of the other dancers, he began to hop. It was difficult, without a doubt. He stumbled, went the wrong way, almost fell in his anxiety. Then, fortified by the pulsating whisky and by the boisterous encouragement of the *Maggie*'s crew, he began to improve. He began to relax. Sheena smiled at him with pleasure. He was enjoying himself!

They danced up and down the hall, missing one couple, hitting another. As they wheeled in a complex manœuvre he happened to catch the Skipper's eyes, and for no reason at all, unless it was the irresistible air of friendship, the whisky, Sheena's youthful charm, he began to laugh. Turning, wheeling, laughing, he saw MacTaggart, the engineman, the mate and the wee boy nodding with approval like a group of benevolent but slightly intoxicated gnomes.

Chapter Twenty-Three

When Sheena ran out into the garden Marshall followed without thinking. He couldn't have explained why. Normally a cautious man, he felt almost light-headed this evening. Irresponsible! Coming sharply from the brightly lit hall into the darkness of the garden he stumbled across the grass, almost fell into a bush.

'Don't run away! Where are you?'

Sheena stopped within sight of the house and leant breathlessly against a low stone wall. She was laughing with happiness and excitement. 'Oh, isn't it a lovely party?'

Marshall diffidently leant against the wall beside her. Round the garden other couples were walking, there was romance in the air. He said uneasily, 'What I can't understand is why you should want to spend the whole evening with me, when all those young fellows . . .'

She said, with a toss of her head, 'Oh, I can always dance with them, and it's exciting to meet a stranger. Not many strange men come to Bellabegwinnie, as you can guess.' She looked at him seriously. 'And you're a very attractive man.'

'I?' He was truly astonished. 'I am?'

'Of course you are.' She glanced up at him slyly. 'Do you think I'm attractive?'

'Well – yes, I do.'

'I'm glad. It will do the two of them good to see that.'

'The two of them? Which two?'

She took his arm and pointed at the hall. 'Look!' He was disturbed to see that two pleasant-faced young men were watching them, one at the door and one at the window. They were obviously trying to hide their anxiety behind a cloak of indifference, but neither was succeeding.

Marshall said, 'I saw them in the hall, while we were dancing. They've been watching you every minute. Who are they?'

She turned her back on them and smiled as she looked up at Marshall. 'The one in the window is Donald Macdougall. He's a fisherman. The one in the door is Ian McCullough, and he owns the store by the pier, and the question is – which should I marry?'

'Oh!'

She said with a charming naïvety, 'It's very difficult, when you're only nineteen, to make such a decision. It would be easier if I were older. I would know so much more – I mean, about men . . .'

Seeing her two suitors waiting so anxiously Marshall thought she wasn't doing too badly. He smiled and asked, 'Well – but how will you choose?'

She said, 'Well, everyone says that Ian should be the one, because he owns the store, and already he is planning to buy another on Colonsay. And people say that Ian McCullough will be a great man one day.'

'And the other? Donald Macdougall?'

Her voice softened. 'He's – just a fisherman, who sails with his brothers, when they're not all drinking or fighting or running after girls. And he hasn't much money. And he's not so handsome as Ian McCullough, everyone agrees to that.'

Marshall raised his hands. 'Well, Sheena, I don't want to influence you, but it doesn't seem a very difficult choice.'

'You mean I should marry Ian?'

'Well, if he's really going to be somebody, if he really wants to make something of himself . . . You'll want a man you know can take care of you and can give you the things you need.'

'Yes . . .' she agreed. 'It would be exciting to be married to a man who will do big things, a man who is going far in the world. And it would be exciting to be taken to places, and to be given fine clothes and expensive presents. I would like all those things. But . . .', she looked up at his face, 'I think it will be the other I'll be taking.'

'But why? I don't understand.'

She explained gently, 'Oh . . . it's simply that, even though he's away with his brothers so much, he'll have more time for me. He'll not be so interested in what he's trying to do, or where he's going to, because – he'll just be fishing. And when he's come home from the fishing – there'll just be me. And when we're very old we'll have only what we have been able to make together for ourselves . . . And I think, perhaps, that is all we'll need.'

The girl stopped as though suddenly embarrassed by the frankness of her simple thoughts. Glancing at him shyly she saw his set, unhappy face and, not understanding, wondered desperately how she could change the subject.

But Marshall was not thinking of Sheena. He could only remember the simple truth she had expounded. At home in London, Lydia fluttered pretty wings about her expensive cage, while her husband, Calvin B. Marshall, the boss man, the success . . .

He shook away his despondency. 'Did you see MacTaggart dancing?'

When they returned to the hall he was glad that she left him, to dance with her young suitors. The revelry, which, by the volume of sound, was now at its height, had lost for him its early sparkle. He moved uneasily towards the table.

'Hello, sir, will ye have another wee dram?'

The music blared, the villagers danced, the glass in his hand seemed to have an inexhaustible amount of whisky.

'What about anither?'

The floor curved, walls swayed; the fiddle fuddled, music incomprehensible . . .

'Hamish, will ye take his other arm? The boy – where's the wee boy? . . . Run on, laddie, and see his bunk's ready.'

Along the darkened wharf, water cool and enticing, the smell of tarred ropes.

'Hold the ladder still. How can ye expect us to get him down!'

As he was being carried across the deck he heard the engineman's gloomy prediction. 'There'll be a thick head here in the morning.'

Chapter Twenty-Four

Marshall came painfully to consciousness with the sour taste of whisky in his mouth and his eyes burning from the sunlight that came glaring down the hatch. He heard what he thought to be the beat of the engine, and it took him some seconds to realise that it was the throbbing of his own head. Carefully he touched his legs, his chest. He was fully clothed. At least he wouldn't have to go through the torture of dressing. For a minute or two, as he waited for his outraged senses to adjust themselves to the day, he had time to wonder why the boat was so quiet: no engine, no tramp of boots. MacTaggart had promised to sail with the dawn tide.

Then he heard somebody coming. He was able to keep his eyes open long enough to see the boy coming carefully down the ladder with a mug of tea. Tea! His stomach turned in protest.

'Good morning, Mr Marshall.'

The American opened his eyes warily. He grunted, sat up too quickly, and had to clasp both hands to his head. 'Oh! Oh!' For a moment, as he swayed through dizziness and pain, he only wanted to die. *Oh, death, where is they sting*? He waved a weak hand at the boy and started to lie down again, but the centre of pain was there, in the hard pillow. He had to sit up. Stunned by suffering he looked vacantly at the boy, who grinned and held out the mug.

'I thought you might like some tea, sir.'

Weakly, he accepted the mug. He took a sip and carefully nodded his thanks. To his surprise his head didn't fall off.

'Where are we?'

The boy said, 'We are still in Bellabegwinnie, sir.'

'In Bella – that place we were in last night?'

'That's right, sir.'

'But it's daylight. In the name of goodness what time is it?' Without moving the position of his head he fumbled for his watch. He looked at it and frowned. 'One o'clock? My watch must have stopped.' He held it to his ear, and his face furrowed with alarm. 'One o'clock! And we're still here! Why aren't we on our way?' With a prodigious effort he swung his feet clear of the bunk. 'What has been happening? Where is everybody?'

As he closed his eyes in pain he heard the boy's non-committal, 'I think they're up in the village, sir.'

With hardly more control of his limbs than he had shown on the previous night the American staggered across the cabin and up the companion ladder to the deck.

'But, sir, don't you think . . . ?'

Marshall said wearily, 'Oh, come on. Let's get this thing organised. Let's get out of here.'

As he came out into the cruel sunlight he had to stop on the ladder, while his tired eyes recovered from the shock.

Sunlight glinting from the water, reflecting from the wharf and the dusty road: the dazzling blue of the sky. He glanced back to the pleasing darkness of the cabin, to the boy, who was watching him anxiously. He said, 'Never, whatever you do, never, never, *never* bring me back to Bellabegwinnie.'

Moving very carefully, like a man crossing a high girder, he tacked across the wharf and up the village street. Someone called him cheerfully, 'Good day to ye, Mr Marshall,' and another, a woman, greeted, 'Good afternoon, sir,' but he was not in a fit state to suffer any diversions. Looking grimly ahead, at the next step and the one beyond that, he made for his objective, the village pub. Someone, probably the boy, was following a few paces away, but he had no reserves of energy or equilibrium to turn round.

The village pub! He heard rather than saw it, for it was still an effort to keep his eyes wide open, and the babble of voices, the chink of glasses, were unmistakable. He stood carefully in the doorway and opened his eyes. The Skipper was coming cheerfully from the bar.

'Good morning to ye, Mr Marshall. Won't ye . . .'

With an irritable gesture Marshall stepped back into the street. As he leant against the wall for support he saw the wee boy standing a few yards away and the Skipper coming through the doorway.

'Won't ye come in and join us, sir? A wee drappie will do ye no harm at all.'

Marshall said emphatically, 'No, no. Let's get going.'

'But ye'll take just one, sir. I'm afraid ye left the celebrations a little abruptly last night, but all ye need is a hair of the dog that bit ye.'

With great restraint, Marshall said, 'Come on MacTaggart. I'm serious.' He turned and walked a few paces, but the Skipper did not follow.

'Well, I'm sorry . . . we cannot go just at the minute, sir.'

Marshall turned back. 'Why not?'

'Well . . . ye see, Hamish is missing somewhere, ever since last night.' He said firmly, 'I am very angry with him, sir, very angry indeed.'

Marshall said with a steely emphasis, 'Then leave him. But let's get out of this place *now*.'

The Skipper shuffled apologetically. 'Well, you see, sir, I thought you wouldna mind, and I told Mr McGregor it would be all right if he went to visit his cousin . . .' He went on, uneasily, as Marshall turned away in fury, 'But it's only a mile away, and he should be back by now, at all events . . .' The innocent explanation tailed off before the American's look of cold fury.

Marshall said, 'All right, MacTaggart, I've had all I can stand. I'm *warning* you! If you don't get on to that boat and get under way right now, I'll . . . I don't know what I'll do, but I'll *ruin* you. I'm warning you. You're going to think a ton of bricks has fallen on you!'

The Skipper said sympathetically, 'Ach, I know how you feel, Mr Marshall, but ye'll be all right when ye've had one or two . . .' He had actually taken the American's arm to lead him back into the pub when he was swung violently away.

'You crazy old fool! You're drunk already!'

Charging down the street in a haze of frustration and fury Marshall came suddenly to the post office. He remembered his humiliation there yesterday and now he went in like a desperate man, determined to stand no nonsense.

'I want to make a telephone call.'

'Where to, sir?' The postmistress was obviously startled by his manner.

'Let me think a minute.' He made a quick decision. 'I want the Central Hotel, Glasgow. I want to speak to a Mr Pusey.'

'All right, sir. That'll cost you . . .'

'I know, I know. I *know*!'

As he stood fuming in the post office he could see the boy still standing outside the pub. The Skipper was not in sight. The afternoon sky was darkening rapidly as storm clouds moved across the sun. The wind was rising, and a few scraps of paper, a cigarette packet, whirled with the moving dust. The engineman came tramping up the street and stopped by the boy, who nodded towards the pub. It seemed that they were both going in to join the Skipper when they saw someone trudging wearily down the road. It was Hamish the mate and he looked as though he had walked a very long way.

Marshall turned angrily from the window. 'Have you got my number yet?'

'Not yet, sir. They're just connecting us.'

He took up the telephone and began in a quiet but fiercely aggressive voice, 'Hello! Pusey? Now listen. I'm in a hurry. I want you to do something for me. Get in touch with – no, don't interrupt, just pay attention. Get in touch with Campbell. Ask for the address of that MacTaggart woman . . . *Look*, Pusey. I don't have time to explain. These maniacs have practically shanghaied me! Pusey, will you listen to what I'm . . . What? What?'

He was aware that the postmistress, fascinated by his lunacy, was listening to every word. She brought in a lamp to combat the sudden darkness and placed it so that it illuminated his haggard face.

Marshall was shouting now. 'What? Who? You mean you're . . . ? Oh, for Heaven's sake! Well, will you put me back to reception, please . . . Hello, reception. Look, incredible as it may seem, you have *two* Mr Puseys staying at your hotel. I want the other one. That's right.' He put his hand to his forehead. 'Two Puseys! Holy smoke!'

Chapter Twenty-Five

The Skipper, the engineman, the mate and the wee boy came in line abreast down the village street. They walked in silence, as though for once their cheerful united front was shaken. The engineman and the boy were worried; the mate was hobbling self-consciously; even the Skipper seemed to be hiding troubled thoughts behind his beard and bushy eyebrows. The storm which had been threatening for the last hour was blowing up in earnest. Heavy clouds rolling across the sun had brought an evening darkness. The street was almost deserted.

The four figures, silhouetted in the gloom, stopped as a fearsome apparition emerged from the post office. Mr Marshall!

The American stood in their path, without speaking, and his eyes, so the wee boy said afterwards, were glowing like a demon's. But it took more than a demon to daunt the Skipper. He advanced confidently, smiling and obviously eager to get on with the job.

'Mr Marshall . . .'

Marshall said, 'All right, MacTaggart, you asked for it right from the word "Go", and now you've got it! I've *bought* your rotten hulk from under you.'

'Ye've what!' The Skipper stared at him, dumbfounded.

'I've bought it, do you understand? The thing belongs to me.' He turned away quickly, as though, perhaps, some kindlier self had spoilt his moment of revenge.

The Skipper stared unbelievingly and then stumbled after him. In a dazed voice he asked, 'Ye've – ye've bought the *Maggie*?'

'That's right.'

'But what are ye – what are ye going to do with her, sir! With a Puffer?'

Marshall came back a few paces. He seemed to bite out his words as he said, 'I'll tell you what I'm going to do. I'm going to take my cargo to Kiltarra! The moment the legal authorisation comes through, I'm moving out of here. I won't have any trouble finding a crew.' He hesitated before their hurt understanding. He shuffled and then, whipping up fresh anger, said, 'You can come or stay here, just as you wish. And when I've got my stuff to Kiltarra, I'm going to sell that – that thing for scrap!'

He turned again and strode down the hill towards the harbour. He had expected them to argue, plead, even threaten, but their stunned silence had taken away all the joy of victory. It really meant something to them.

A scrawny chicken ran squawking before his angry steps, and a dog slunk through a half-open doorway. By golly, he had reason to be angry! Could any man put up with more than he had suffered? What it had cost already in precious hours was something he tried not to think about; what it had cost in hard cash was a worry for his accountant. They had been definitely dishonest. A harder man would have had them in jail. MacTaggart was a lunatic and a crook, his crew amiable thugs!

When he reached the *Maggie* he looked back, expecting them to have followed him down the hill, but they were still standing where he had left them. In the gathering gloom he could just discern their shadowy outlines: the Skipper, a figure of tragedy, leaning against the sea wall, the engine man and the mate watching him from the road. And apart, like a sprite in the reflected light of the post office, the wee boy was standing with feet astride, looking down at the harbour.

Marshall clambered angrily on to the boat and went down into the cabin. He opened his briefcase and scattered some papers across the table. Crooks! Prison was the place for them! If anything, he had been too lenient.

He settled down to his papers, but somehow his brain wouldn't stay in the correct grooves. He reached automatically across the table for a telephone and then, remembering where he was, fell to brooding once more. Crooks! Lunatics!

He started guiltily as he heard someone walking across the deck. A slow light tread: the Skipper? But it was the boy who came down the companion ladder. Marshall bent busily over his papers.

'Mr Marshall, sir . . .' Marshall looked up at the boy's reproachful face. The boy said gently, 'Ye canna do it, sir.'

'I'm sorry, Douggie.' The American squirmed before his small inquisitor. Then, as he remembered once more all that he had suffered, he leapt to his feet in a sudden onrush of frustration and fury. His briefcase and the papers spilled across the floor. 'Look, I'm tired of all this. I'm not *interested* in MacTaggart and his problems. I have enough of my own. And I don't care what *you* think of him, the man is nothing better than a crook!'

The boy's lip came out mulishly: 'He's no'!'

Marshall knelt to gather the spilled papers. 'He's a petty thief!'

'He's no'!' The boy, trembling with outraged loyalty, was nervously fingering the catch which held up the heavy teak table hinged to the wall.

Marshall was saying. 'Above all he's a *liar*. Don't you understand that?'

The boy's expression changed from doggedness to a new fearful hope as he realised the possibilities of the catch.

'He lied and lied and lied,' Marshall was saying. 'There's not a trick in the book that he hasn't used . . .'

The boy swallowed twice.

'. . . Well, he's pulled his last trick on me. He . . .'

With the smallest of gestures and with an expression of sorrow rather than anger, the boy pulled the catch. The heavy table fell with a sickening thud, and Marshall's voice died in his throat.

The crew of the *Maggie*, a small group of pathetic, defeated, bewildered men, were still standing near the post office as the boy trudged slowly up the hill. Only the mate turned to face him as he approached.

The boy licked his lips and swallowed. 'Hamish!'

'Aye?'

'Ye better go aboard. I think I've killed him.'

Chapter Twenty-Six

(I)

The wee boy sat on a bollard watching the lighted hatch of the captain's cabin. Below him, on the deck, McGregor and Hamish were waiting anxiously and in silence. Securely wrapped by darkness the boy had time to think of what he had done. The deliberate moving of the catch, the heavy table: the police would only call it one thing – murder. He was quite sure that Marshall would die. Against the stiffening wind the boat rose and fell, rose and fell. The choppy waves slapped her bottom as she rubbed skittishly against the pier. The good old *Maggie*. The boy clenched his fists. He wasn't sorry for what he had done. A man who would sell her to the breaker's yard deserved all that was coming to him – even a ship's heavy table. He wondered tearfully whether the Skipper would come to see him in the condemned cell.

He leant forward as a head appeared in the hatchway; the engineman and the mate rushed forward. 'Is he all right?'

The Skipper, who was first up the companion ladder, did not answer. He turned to assist the doctor, an elderly little man, who in spite of twenty years in a fishing village was still a landsman at heart. The doctor's voice, distorted by the wind, gave a reprieve '. . . Nothing to worry about, but he must rest. I've given him a strong sedative. He won't waken till morning.'

McGregor and Hamish embraced in the darkness, and the Skipper, coming up on to the pier with the doctor, raised his thumb. Only the boy showed no obvious signs of relief. If the *Maggie* was really to be sold . . .

The Skipper bade a thankful farewell to the doctor. 'Goodbye to ye, doctor. We're greatly obliged . . .' And as the little man trod carefully along the dark pier the engine-man added his own note of relief, 'And good luck to ye, sir!'

'Well!' They looked at each other happily. That was one nightmare disposed of. The Skipper, understanding more than was apparent from his innocent countenance, touched the boy on the shoulder. He said, 'Well, laddie, there's no need for ye to worry any more. Mr Marshall will be all right.'

'Is he still going to sell the *Maggie*?'

'Well . . .' the Skipper added, with characteristic confidence, 'he'll no' be able to think about that tonight, nor yet tomorrow. Maybe he'll forget . . .'

As if to refute his easy assurance the gaunt figure of the postmistress was coming along the pier. They heard her frigid greeting, 'Good night, doctor,' and then she was bearing down on them, ready to destroy their new-found gaiety. She passed the boy, who was still sitting on the bollard, and would have passed the Skipper if she had not been afraid of the uncertain climb down to the deck. She said, 'I've a telegram . . .' and, snatching it from the Skipper's grasp, 'for Mr Marshall'.

'He's a sick man,' the Skipper said. 'He'll no' be fit . . . Ye'd better give it to me.'

For a moment it seemed as though she would demand to see the body before she departed from the strict line of duty. Then she asked, 'Marshall . . . is that yon phoning body?'

'Aye.'

She thrust the envelope into the Skipper's hands. 'Ye can take it – and welcome!'

As she went with her disapproval into the darkness the Skipper held up the telegram, as though by the feel of it or the texture of the paper he could read what was inside. He looked down at the engineman and the mate. Then he shrugged and said in a hopeless voice, 'I suppose it's all right for me to open it – if it's from me own sister.'

Tearing slowly and hesitantly with his forefinger he opened the envelope. He unfolded the paper and held it close to his eyes while the crew waited in dreadful suspense. 'I can't make out . . .' Even under the pier lamp the light wasn't good.

Then, as he read and understood, his expression changed. They saw him staring incredulously, as though the news was even worse than he had expected.

He said, in an awestruck voice, 'It's no' from Sarah. It's from Pusey. He says, "She refuses to sell under any circumstances. Stop. What are your instructions?"'

They were too amazed to feel the rising tide of gladness. The boy had jumped to his feet. 'She wouldna sell.'

Then, after the first shock, the Skipper was ready to snap at opportunity. He beat a clenched fist into his open palm. There was excitement now in his voice as he said, 'With any luck we can have him in Kiltarra by the time he wakes up.' He climbed nimbly down the ladder. 'We'd best get under way.'

(2)

The *Maggie* nosed fussily through the comparatively calm water of the harbour and made for the open sea. There was a stiff wind blowing, and the white combers showed clearly in the darkness ahead. Angry-looking clouds were racing across the sky, but in the brief intervals of moonlight the forbidding coastline, the rising mountains, showed above the stern, and a few lights were all that could be seen of Bellabegwinnie.

As they came out into the Atlantic they met the real weather, the wind, driving spray, a heavy swell. The *Maggie* lurched, tossed, and then, shaking herself clear of water, butted gamely into the next heavy wave. In the wheelhouse the Skipper and the mate were poring over crumpled charts. By the uncertain light of an oil lamp they plotted their course. Bellabegwinnie to Kiltarra. 'With luck,' the Skipper shouted, 'we'll be there in the morning,' repeating for his own confidence the assurance he had given on the pier.

In the engine-room McGregor was sweating blasphemously: open door, red-hot furnace, long shovel: stoke her up, stoke her up. 'Give her everything you've got,' the Skipper had said. 'Let's see what she can do.' McGregor slammed the furnace door. If that was what he wanted! He felt a part of the machinery and drew his hand away quickly. Glowering, he ministered with his oil-can. Six knots, he wanted – as if she'd do it! He took up his shovel.

In the bows the boy was alone and happy. The white line of the waves rose and fell as the ship tossed. Wind and spray were stinging his face. Breathing contentment he turned and glanced up at the sky. He saw the mast rolling with an odd kind of dignity and the patchy clouds scudding across the heavens.

Through the night they battled westward in rough seas. Only the American, asleep in the cabin, missed the excitement and urgency of their voyage. Towards dawn the tide turned, but the wind and the waves were as strong as ever. Sometimes, as she sank into a deep trough, it seemed that the *Maggie* would never recover. It was a miracle that she had not submerged, a miracle repeated a hundred times that night.

Dawn broke behind them, with a few grey pennants of light across the streaky sky. Above the howling wind they could hear a new sound, the roar of surf against rocks, and, as the light grew stronger, they could see the white foam some distance away to starboard.

The Skipper looked at his watch and nudged the mate to take the wheel. With oilskins flattened against his legs, the spray whipping coldly on his face, he traversed the heaving deck to the engine-room hatch. It was true that he had been born on the *Maggie*, and now sixty years later he knew the feel of every inch of her, and in every kind of weather. She was so much a part of him that he could feel in the heartbeat from the engine-room that she wasn't going well. He stood with his hands gripping the hatch and his head bent forward, listening. He went crab-wise down the steps.

'She's no soundin' so well.'

The engineman looked up from the coal bunker and scowled. 'Haven't I always been telling ye? Ye'll no' spend a penny to get her boilers cleaned . . .'

The Skipper was worried. 'Can ye hear anything?'

'Hear anything! She's going the same as she always has – considering she's not had a penny spent on maintenance, not a spanner, not even an oily rag . . .'

The Skipper could never be worried for long. He said optimistically as he climbed the ladder; 'Ah weel, in half an hour it'll be daylight. We'll be nearly to Kiltarra.'

As he came out into the blustery dawn the boy met him with a steaming cup of tea.

'Thanks, laddie. There's nothing like a good cup of tea.'

He climbed down the companion ladder into his own cabin. Without releasing his grip on the ladder he could see the small stuffy cabin: the table (folded to the wall now), the glass of medicine, the folded clothes. In the bunk Marshall was sleeping peacefully.

(3)

But the Skipper was wrong. As he climbed quietly back on to the deck the man in the bunk opened his eyes. He too was listening to the heavy, slightly irregular beat of the engine.

His expression was oddly quiet and thoughtful. So much had happened since he had decided to send his precious cargo to Kiltarra. From the pitch of the boat and the early sunlight filtering down the hatch he guessed that the journey was nearly over. Glasgow to Kiltarra; some furniture, building material, a boiler: not a difficult order, by any means, and yet . . . So much had happened; so much had changed. Lydia, Pusey, the girl Sheena. He realised how MacTaggart and his crew had come like spirits into his well-ordered life, how they had shaken him from his complacency until now he wasn't sure of anything any more, not even of himself.

He rose carefully on one elbow and propped a pillow behind his back. The sunlight was brighter now, but the wind was still blowing strongly enough to throw the boat up and down, backwards and forwards, until he felt drowsy again with the swaying. Would Lydia be at Kiltarra?

More feet were coming down the companion ladder: the mate. Finding the passenger awake, Hamish assumed a transparent air of heartiness.

'How are ye, Mr Marshall? I'm afraid ye had a nasty accident.' He fingered the table and was obviously embarrassed by the necessary lie. 'The table must have been . . .'

Marshall asked quietly, 'Is Douggie aboard?' When the mate hesitated he said, 'Tell him I want to see him.'

The mate turned doubtfully towards the companion ladder. He made as if to speak and then thought better of it. He climbed up on to the deck.

Marshall rose, feeling his head gingerly, and tried to look out of the porthole. He heard the faint voices on deck: 'He's awake. He wants to see Douggie.'

'No, I'll no' see him.'

And then the Skipper's voice, 'It's all right, lad. Ye'd better go.'

In a few minutes the boy came slowly down the ladder. At the bottom he turned and faced Marshall.

Marshall said quietly, 'You might have killed me, Douggie.'

The boy watched him with dour wariness.

'Did you hear what I said? You might have killed me. Why?'

'Ye were taking the *Maggie* away from the Captain.'

'I'd every right to buy this . . .'

The boy interrupted passionately, 'Ye did not. And anyway, there was a telegram . . . The Captain's sister wouldna sell it to ye!'

'Wouldn't sell!' Marshall saw from the boy's look of grim satisfaction that he was telling the truth. He asked, 'Why not?'

'Ach, ye wouldn't understand.'

Marshall put a hand to his aching head. He asked weakly, 'How soon do we get in?'

'An hour, maybe.' As conscience struggled with loyalty the boy flared out, 'Ye were going to leave the Captain ashore without his ship. Ye didn't care what happened to him, an old man . . .'

Marshall protested indignantly, 'Well, did he care at all what happened to my cargo?'

'He got ye here, didn't he?'

'After seven days and nights of . . .'

'Ye were going to take his *ship*,' the boy interrupted,

almost in tears. He hesitated, then added guiltily, 'I'm sorry for what happened.'

'You are?'

'Aye.' Then with another touch of belligerence, 'But I'd do it again. The Captain may have been slow in getting your cargo to Kiltarra for ye, and ye may not think much of his boat . . . and maybe he's *not* the best skipper in the coastal trade like I said. But it was no reason to do what ye did. No reason at all.'

Chapter Twenty-Seven

Some minutes had passed before Marshall realised that the engine had stopped. He was vaguely conscious that the boy had run up on to the deck and that somewhere alongside voices were raised in violent argument. The boy's unexpected condemnation was, he knew, a condemnation of all his ideals, of money, efficiency, success. He had learnt so much in these few days.

Slowly the unexpected silence broke through his thoughts. The heavy engine beat was gone, the rhythmic throb that had lulled him through the night. Now there was only the engineman's voice clashing with the Skipper's, while the boat, wallowing in the heavy sea, seemed to be going in all directions at once. Marshall put his head against the partition to hear what the argument was about in the engine-room. He could hear the engineman's voice, raised in passion, and a steady clang of metal against metal as though he was emphasising each point with a spanner.

'Ye wouldna listen! Look at it! Look at the eccentric rod!' Clang. 'We'll never get it straight!' Clang. 'Ye wouldna spend a penny!' Clang.

And then the Skipper, trying to be conciliatory but having to shout above the din: 'Why has she seized? Robbie, what is it? Ye forgot to put oil on the straps!'

'Put oil on the straps! Is it me ye're blaming!' Clang. 'Look at the motion! Holy smoke, how d'ye expect me to do anything?' Clang. 'We're sunk.' Clang. 'I tell ye we're sunk! Ye may as well abandon ship right now!'

'Will ye listen?' The Skipper was bawling. 'Will ye listen? We're in dangerous waters, Robbie. Ye've got to get it repaired! Shut up your blethering! Try what ye can do!'

There was a violent clatter as though a spanner – a whole box of spanners – had been flung at the silent engine. Then McGregor's voice came again, in panic: 'I'm coming up. I'll no' stay down here. No waste, no paraffin, no tools! Get out of my way, ye old goat! I canna do anything about it.'

And the Skipper's plaintive cry, 'Have ye gone daft? I'll no' abandon ship. Will ye listen?'

Marshall climbed unhurriedly on deck and walked straight into the Skipper, who was scrambling from the engine-room hatch. For a moment they clutched each other for support and the Skipper, in absolute panic now, shouted, 'There's no cause for alarm, sir. No cause whatever.'

Marshall held him firmly by the shoulder. 'What's the matter? What's wrong with the engine?'

'He forgot to put oil on the straps . . .' The old man was too upset to think coherently. The boy was still and silent by the hatchway, and the mate was glancing uneasily at the reef.

Marshall saw it then, lines of jagged rocks against which the waves were pounding with cascades of spray and an undertow of white foam. The sullen roaring of the surf could be plainly heard, and it was obvious, with even the most casual glance, that the *Maggie* was drifting to her doom.

Marshall asked again, 'What's wrong with the engine?'

He was answered by the engineman, who came scrambling for the hatch, only to fall heavily on the slippery deck. He rose disgustedly, rubbing his buttocks. 'Ach, it's the eccentric rod. It's no' worth the . . .'

Marshall asked sharply, 'Well, can't you fix it?'

'It's no use trying. I hav'na the tools.'

Marshall pushed past him and began to clamber down into the engine-room. There was no cause to doubt McGregor's word. The rod was indeed eccentric. It had a distinct bend.

The engineman, thrusting his head into the hatch, called, 'Ach, she's finished. It's no use. We haven't anything we need. No tools, no . . .'

Marshall was already examining the eccentric rod with professional eyes. He felt it, estimating the strength they would need to get it straight. He turned over the miserable collection of tools.

'This'll do.' He held up a turning bar. 'Now run and get some wedges.'

The engineman began, 'What do you want wedges . . . ?'

'Get some wedges, you nitwit! Don't just stand there.'

Up on deck the Skipper was in control of himself again. He was standing at the wheel, but there was nothing he could do except to stare at the roaring, seething, relent-lessly-approaching line of rocks. Then, with destruction only a hundred yards away, he began to relax. He even gave a little optimistic smile. Mr Marshall was an engineer. Maybe he'd fix it!

Marshall was indeed fixing it. He had fitted the wedges so that he could get a full leverage on the eccentric rod with the turning bar. In a state of semi-hysteria the engine-man was holding the wedges which Marshall was using as a fulcrum. The engineman was complaining, 'Ach, I told him. He wouldna do anything I ask. The boiler hasna been cleaned in nearly a year. She's showing salt everywhere, look at it! All the boiler valves are leaking . . .'

Straining at the bar, Marshall ordered, 'Hold those wedges!'

'He never gives me any waste or paraffin. The slice and the rake are almost burned away. And look at the fire-bars! I've got coal dripping into the ashpit! I've got no soap and soda, not even a decent chisel! And ye ought to hear what Hamish says: all the mooring ropes are falling to pieces, even the ratlings are gone. And the bogey-fun-nel smokes, ye can't even eat decent. The spanners don't fit, we never get any paint. It's as much as he'll do to . . .' He broke off in astonishment as the rod began to give. Marshall was bearing down on it with all his strength. It was coming straight!

The engineman said, 'She'll break! She'll come to pieces! Ye'll never do it! Ye'll put the whole engine apart!'

Before he had finished speaking the rod was straight. Breathing heavily, Marshall threw down the turning bar and stood up. 'Now then, which is the main gear lever? Where . . .'

He was flung violently forward as the whole engine-room tilted and shuddered. There was a tremendous grating noise from the bows and the deafening roar of surf. The *Maggie* was on the rocks.

Chapter Twenty-Eight

As Marshall scrambled on to the deck it seemed for a moment that the others had already abandoned ship. Then out of the scuppers rose the mate, followed by the wee boy. They looked at each other, aghast. The boy turned and, slipping on the steeply tilted deck, clambered up to the wheelhouse.

As he pulled open the door they saw the dazed face of the Skipper, who was sprawling in an ungainly position, below the level of the windows.

'Are ye all right, Captain, sir?'

Marshall joined the mate, who was leaning over the bulwarks. On the landward side the sea was comparatively calm.

'Is she badly damaged?'

'Ach, no sir – not yet. It's when the tide comes in.'

The Skipper came slowly back to join them. For the first time Marshall saw him as an old man. The spirit had gone, and he looked tired and haggard as he stood gripping the rail and watching the triumphant seas breaking over the *Maggie*. From the slope of the deck it was apparent that she was down by the stern, with her bows clear of the water. She was leaning sideways so that to cross from the bulwarks to the hatchway was like walking up a steep hill.

The Skipper said, 'I'm sorry, sir, that this should have happened at the last.'

'It's all right.'

'At least ye'll be able to get ashore. I'll have the dinghy lowered.' His grey beard settled on his chest and his brows jutted in despair. 'Your cargo'll be safe enough, sir. When ye get ashore ye'll be able to get to Kiltarra within half an hour. Ye can make arrangements for another boat to come alongside us and trans-ship. Ye've got twelve hours and there's plenty of craft about.'

The crew were already lowering the dinghy. The derrick reaching out from the side gave an impression of stability like the pole of a tightrope walker, but the *Maggie* was still shuddering at each wave.

Marshall did not move towards the dinghy. He asked, 'But what happens when the next tide comes in?'

The Skipper shook his head and smiled, as though apologising for the *Maggie*'s frailty. 'Ach, she'll no' be able to take *that* sort of punishment. It'll break her back.' He put his hand to his eyes and said with a touching air of pride, 'Well, we got ye within five miles of Kiltarra, sir. It wasna too bad for an old Puffer.'

Marshall looked past him – to the crew who were waiting by the dinghy. He said, 'And what if you jettison the cargo?'

'Sir?' The Skipper was startled.

'What if you throw it over?'

'But ye canna do that, sir. Ye canna . . .'

Marshall said impatiently, 'Just answer the question.'

The Skipper stroked his beard. 'Well, she's near on high tide. If the wind held outside, the tide might no' go away. We might have a chance.' He looked straight at Marshall and frowned. 'But ye canna be serious, man. It cost ye a lot more than what the boat is worth.'

Marshall squared his shoulders. 'All right. Throw it over!'

He turned to face the engineman, the mate and the wee boy, who were looking at him in wonder. He said, 'Don't worry. It was bound to happen. It was all that was left that *could* happen.'

The Skipper argued querulously, 'But, Mr Marshall, it cost ye over . . .'

'Don't tell me how much it cost,' Marshall said. 'Just throw the damn stuff over!'

They stared at him for a minute, as though considering his sanity, and then leapt to obey his command. The boy swung down into the hold, the engineman ran to the winch.

The first big crate, labelled Calvin B. Marshall, jerked and rose from its frame as the derrick hook pulled on its cords. It swung clear of the deck and was lowered to rest on the bulwark just in front of Marshall.

The American stared at it grimly. So many hopes, so much planning, to be thrown overboard to satisfy a whim! But if he felt any doubts at that point they were settled by the sight of the boy clambering up from the hold. The boy looked at him with eyes which showed gratitude and admiration, and then, seeing the huge expensive crate, turned to plant himself squarely in front of the Skipper.

Noticing the Skipper's obvious embarrassment Marshall wondered what would happen next – what *could* happen? The Skipper shuffled, as though anxious to sidestep his responsibility, but then, unable to shake off the boy's compelling stare, he came sheepishly forward to the rail. He cleared his throat loudly.

'There's just one thing I forgot to tell ye, sir.'

Marshall waited with a blank mind.

'What with one thing and another, sir, I'm afraid we never got to the business of insuring the cargo.'

Marshall did not look at the Skipper. He was watching the crate poised on the bulwark. Was it worth it? Could anything justify such an expensive gesture? The *Maggie* groaned and shifted slightly as she settled more heavily on the rocks. The Skipper gave a deep sigh as though he had heard the death rattle of an old and dear friend. Marshall turned slowly and took one pace forward so that he was directly in front of the Skipper. He said, 'MacTaggart, I want you to understand one thing, and I'm serious. . . . If you laugh at me for this, I swear I'll kill you with my bare hands.'

He turned savagely to the mate. 'Throw it over!'

In a fury of impatience he heard the winch lowering the derrick. The mate began to unfasten the hook. 'Here!' Marshall couldn't bear the suspense. He struggled with the hook until it was clear of the rope, and then heaved desperately until the crate toppled over-board into the sea. They all looked down as the seething waters splashed and then closed over it as it sank to the ocean bed.

Chapter Twenty-Nine

(1)

The arrival of the *Maggie* at Glenbrashan caused something of a sensation. As Pusey came running down the hill from the hotel he passed several groups of villagers, all making for the pier. Pusey was nervous and spectacularly upset. He couldn't understand what had happened, but, whatever it was, he felt that he would be blamed. Trotting at his shoulder was the reporter, still wiping the traces of an interrupted breakfast from his mouth. Pusey was complaining to himself, 'I don't understand. I don't *understand*.'

As he came down to the harbour he saw that the *Maggie* was already tied up at the pier. He trotted out, like a worried hen, and stared down into the empty hold.

'The cargo! Mr Marshall!'

He stumbled towards the wheelhouse, passing close to three members of the crew. He shouted across to the Skipper, 'What's happened? Where's Mr Marshall?'

The Skipper jerked his thumb towards the three men he had just passed. Pusey stared unbelievingly at the man he had not recognised – dressed in blue seaman's clothes, unshaven, and with wild hair.

'Mr Marshall!'

Marshall asked, 'Is my wife here?'

'She's up at the hotel, sir.'

Marshall stared up at a large house on a promontory overlooking the harbour. He had arrived at last. Several villagers were watching him from the end of the pier, and a man was coming forward with a curious air of respect. It was the reporter, Fraser.

'Mr Marshall . . .' The reporter stopped, noticing the empty hold. He turned questioningly. 'They sent me to try to find a pay-off to the story, sir, but this is really something. What happened?'

Marshall shrugged. 'Don't ask me. *I* couldn't tell you.'

The Skipper, the engineman and the mate were grouped, somewhat ceremoniously, across the pier, with the boy sitting apart, on a bollard. The Skipper, plainly nervous, raucously cleared his throat.

'Well?'

The Skipper began, 'Mr Marshall, there was just one small problem, if you could give us your opinion on it.' He hesitated and wetted his lips. 'Apart from expressing our appreciation . . . for what ye . . . uh . . .'

Marshall waved his hand, anxious to get away. 'That's all right, MacTaggart. Forget it.'

The Skipper continued, 'Well, we was wondering, sir, as there was some misunderstanding about whether we should have carried the cargo in the first place, and as – due to various circumstances – we took somewhat longer than we planned in getting to Kiltarra, and as unfortunately we didn't insure the cargo, and – especially as the cargo is all lying at the bottom of the sea . . .'

'Well?'

Slowly, reluctantly, the Skipper took out his wallet. 'We was wondering, sir, if perhaps ye might feel er, er . . . it would be right to – er, to offer to give ye your – er – money back . . .'

Marshall said firmly and affably, 'MacTaggart, in the seven days I've known you that's the first thing you've said that made any sense.'

The Skipper, who had the cheque half out of his wallet, seemed absolutely stunned. He swallowed deeply and put the cheque into Marshall's outstretched hand. There were real tears in his eyes as he watched it go.

Then, unexpectedly, the boy spoke up: 'Ach, if ye're no' going to pay us for doing the job, so we can get our plates put right, why didn't ye just let her sink on the rocks? Ye might as well.'

They were silent as they considered the wee boy's analysis of the basic logic of the situation. Marshall turned to him, wanting to explain but finding no words. He waved his hand helplessly, turned as if for help to the grinning reporter, and then, utterly defeated, handed the cheque back to the Skipper.

The next minute he was overwhelmed with good wishes. The Skipper said with emotion, 'It's been a great pleasure to have been associated with ye, sir. We'll never forget ye.'

The mate took his hand. 'I hope we'll meet ye again, sir.'

Above it all the engineman said, 'Aye, and if ye're ever wanting another job done . . .'

Marshall looked at him closely, but he seemed quite sincere. He nodded and started to walk away.

'Goodbye, Mr Marshall.' Their warm farewells followed him down the pier.

'And gude luck to ye.' The boy's cheerful, faintly derisive call was like a blow on the back. Marshall stopped and turned. Without altering his bland expression the boy met Marshall's hard and speculative stare. For a few moments they looked at each other in silence. Then, somewhere behind the eyes, the boy smiled, and, with only the faintest movement of his lips, Marshall returned the smile. He turned reluctantly and, with one last look at the *Maggie*, started up the steep hill to the hotel.

(2)

The landlord of Dirty Dan's was drying a glass tankard on his apron as he looked out over the docks. It was a typical grey day in Glasgow, with a lowering sky almost touching, it seemed, the high tops of the cranes, the masts of the liners, the tall warehouses. On the placid water all kinds of boats were floating – at anchor, in the repair basin, chugging across the river, coming thankfully in from the sea. The smoke from a dozen funnels hung in the heavy atmosphere, the seagulls whirled, a drizzle of rain was falling.

The landlord came idly to the window as another, smaller, vessel came in from the sea. A Puffer. He turned, grinning, to his only customer, Skipper Anderson of the CSS.

'There's an old Puffer coming in.'

'Aye?' Anderson's voice was non-committal. He was halfway through the latest murder case.

'It wouldn't be the *Maggie*, I'm thinking,' the landlord added wistfully. 'I always hoped she'd come back.'

'What for?'

The landlord shrugged. 'Oh, I don't know. Maybe to hear the whole story – as MacTaggart tells it.'

Captain Anderson put down his newspaper and chuckled. 'Aye, it was a good story – MacTaggart at his best. It's a wonder he didn't end up in jail.'

'He will yet.'

Anderson laughed tolerantly. 'Ah, well, MacTaggart's a real character. Ye'll not find many like him these days.'

The landlord nodded as he arranged the tankards in neat rows at the back of the bar. It was early yet. In another hour the dockyard hooter would go, and he wouldn't be able to fill them quickly enough. By the time he had done this and mopped the polished counter the Puffer was directly below, hardly a stone's throw from his bar. He watched her with mild interest. The window of the wheelhouse was misted over and he couldn't see the captain or the crew. But the name was clear enough, painted in large and rather sloppy lettering along the side. The landlord picked up a pair of binoculars he always kept beneath the bar. He asked in a puzzled voice, 'Have you ever heard of a Puffer called . . .' he pronounced each word slowly – 'the CALVIN B. MARSHALL?'